DOWN FROM THE STARS

Also by John Fraser
and published by AESOP Modern:

Animal Tales
Black Masks
Blue Light / Starting Over
The Case
Enterprising Women
Hard Places
An Illusion of Sun
The Magnificent Wurlitzer
Medusa
Military Roads
The Observatory
The Other Shore
The Red Tank
Runners
Soft Landing
The Storm
Three Beauties
Wayfaring

DOWN FROM THE STARS

JOHN FRASER

AESOP Modern Fiction
Oxford

AESOP Modern Fiction
An imprint of AESOP Publications
Martin Noble Editorial / AESOP
28 Abberbury Road, Oxford OX4 4ES, UK
www.aesopbooks.com

First hardback edition published by AESOP Publications
Copyright (c) 2013 John Fraser
First paperback edition published by AESOP
Publications
Copyright (c) 2014 John Fraser

www.johnfraser.info

A catalogue record of this book is
available from the British Library.

ISBN: 978-0-9927588-6-8

DOWN FROM THE STARS

'I've concluded you're a crook,' says Alessia.

'That's a thing you pick up,' he says. 'It's only saying less than you actually do.'

'I'm off to help people,' she says. 'What'll you do? Fish ideas, dole out other people's art?'

'It's not warm, like blankets,' he says. 'But there's no set price, so some comes cheap.'

'Hedonism? Commitment?' he wonders aloud: 'What's for me?'

There's Alessia, stretched out on a rug, fit as a wolf, her yellow eyes dwell on her future.

Alessia says, 'That's old stuff. Look how they're doing. What they call research. Brains; beginning and end of the world; robot people; empires on other stars. They've gone into them all. It should be clear they know something, cover it up. It's the last spurt. Who cares now, if you burn, or you burn things down? Imagining the big catastrophe – it's an alibi, absolution, for all the other things that's being done, the public and the private ones.'

'Fresh pastures,' he says, 'for you, Alessia.'

'You mean I'm a sheep?' she asks, not coyly. Stern rote, perhaps. Sheep's not so bad. There's cows, and goats.

'There's something biblical about you,' he says. 'But then, that's a book where there's everything in, all hugger-mugger soldiering. Racism galore. Sacrifice maybe, for you – holding high the knife, waiting for the countermand.'

'You mean there's something bossing me?' She gets crosser.

'You could just leave, and no wordplay,' he says. 'But it makes a mock of what was between us.'

'It's just perspective,' she says kindly. 'When there's two of you, there's three or really four and cousins too. When you're alone, you see if you want another. A missing part.'

He's had times of blame, for being the most moderate of the extremists. Now those terms are meaningless. Determined foreigners, gave a charge to us, they read the books, went home to Africa and were corrupt.

'You look like a wolf,' he says to her. 'A husky dog. You're all *en brosse*.'

'It's a myth,' she says, 'about dogs' loyalty. They stick around. They have in mind the quest.'

This leads nowhere.

'Bed?' he asks. 'At the last?'

Her mouth is closed. No.

She says, 'We see the beauty of the life we eat. Food – it saddens you, but puffs you up. You won't let it be, its glory, its heedless thrust. Eat, eat, is you.'

He says, 'My folk used to sacrifice a sheep. It was for God; a present. Of course, we ate the profane bits. But it was life too, to bring something for the big guy, they said, showing we thought He had an appetite. I hope the sheep believed. Me – I don't believe in it, not anything, not parents, not the fire, the knife. The family did. Believed in everything. Your mystical side, Alessia, the beauty stuff. It's new to me. And you're right. Sardines – a marvel. You wouldn't make one if you could. They're just right as they are, food, exploring and comradely.'

'God sniffs the smoke. There's lots around. Beauty comes to mind, it's sentiment – it's because I shan't come back,' Alessia says, 'and I'm leaving you behind.'

'I shan't miss you,' he says. 'Now you're here, and this is you. When you're gone, there's nothing. Of you, not a thing.'

She laughs, 'Brave little soldiers, all of us. Sardines in our can.'

'That's depression,' he says.

'No, no. Just sad.'

'Don't expect thanks out there,' he says. 'People in need thank their neighbours, not their saviours.'

'I don't want a compact with anyone,' she says. 'Not these societies that fell down. Absolutely not. I won't save – just plaster over. No one will tell me stories.'

'Well, if that's enough...' he says.

'It's something. I leave the adventure to you.'

'Remember,' he says, 'shoot the bad guys. Think of payday.'

Their guns are issued when they get on the train. She clumps off down the stairs. She's never seen again – at least, not round here.

There's military everywhere. You go outside, there's spies and uniforms. History running out the troughs and fountains, holes in everything, we float on, like a plank.

'All here's public property,' says a guy. 'So you can't steal for yourself. You can't have private stuff. If you steal, it must have gone to set up your clique.'

We've taken over what no one wanted. Trash that's too heavy and grey to lift away.

Those two – that 'he', Alessia: both dead on her battlefield.

It's the past; to call it 'my past' would be exaggeration. Enough of the 'he'. Now it's 'me', it's 'I'.

A woman I was with, not Jewish, not at all, no need nor wish to shoot at Arabs, went off to be a soldier. It's a romantic comedy, Schlock. I've no loyalty to her, Alessia the soldier, doing without her like you do without a flag, a trumpet.

LESSONS OF THE MASTER

'OK. This is a stinker. Remember, you wanted me to tell you if I thought it. Your idea stinks.'

'I didn't want it told like that,' I say.

The old guy says, 'Einstein left his brain to be cut up. If quantum's right, each slice could have been a pain excruciating.' He settles back. These old guys always laugh when talking quantum. Maybe by thought you add some q-bits to your stature, and I grin. What has he in mind for his, his brain? Sliced, frozen, boiled, or left in vaults. He goes on,

'Maybe you watch too much TV. Some of your thoughts are not original. They're musty. You've not been my assistant long, others were sharper...' and he names some names, as if they're my contemporaries, as if it's my memory that's gone opaque.

11

'Want some moments in the cosmos?' he asks.

'Sure!' I say. There's equations on a membrane, and you push through, there in the light and dark you are, looking up and down. It's empty black, and nests of light – it hurts, it's busy like a gut with particles, your twin is jigging up and down, and so are you. I think, the first dog, sent up or down – Laika was its name, perhaps; I had some cigarettes, the packet had his handsome face – 'Oh no,' the dog thinks, looking out – 'those bastards didn't let me have a window, but I guess it's like the pictures...'

The dog thinks how it's getting hot. It's nearly frying time, he thinks. And then – the dog shouts, 'Jesus, I'm burning up, right up!'

I scream, but here, I'm not sure if it carries, and the old guy wanders in, into my space, he says, 'Now, now, no bad thoughts, they're as irrelevant here as good ones. Just enjoy the view,' but fuck it, it's all quantum, it's all Dum and Dee, and ropes like snakes of infinite length and cunning too, and tiny diddly things that's all your first love was, and canyons just a haze of dust.

'Well,' the guy says. 'That's enough reality, it's quite upset you, like it always does. Let's take a rest from cosmic things.'

What's next – intimacy, or he fires me?

'You see,' he says, 'we physicists – and you will never find yourself among us, sadly – we're not much loved. By women, if we're hetero, by others, if we're not. It's the walking through the stars. Those nebulae – they burn a hole in you. The littlest things, they eat the bodies, and the form's retained, but it's a swirl of maggots, lice, of tiny brothers mirrored in each other. Sexually, we're predators, we tear and mangle. It's just warm matter, and it nourishes, but there's no meal, it's flies that eat the shit, then shit. Of course,' he chuckles, 'you can dress it up a bit. But wandering through the galaxies, and knowing what they're made of – you know what people think that makes us?'

'No.'

'Aliens. Monsters. Magicians.'

'Maybe I wouldn't get that far. I might have other interests,' I say.

'I fear that's true,' he says. 'When we stand out there, on that invisible steel, those bridges to nowhere – we're the only living things. The rest is latent. Strings, and heat. The heat warms you for ever – and all the rest you must scrabble for, and seize. With these.'

He shows me his grey nails, the fingerless mittens.

He's old. They threw him out his job – but that's not striking, it's not what comes to mind – no, it's being alien, a monster, fantasist and predator.

I say, 'I don't have the attack-dog mentality. I
can't savage lambs like you. I'm not predatory. Maybe
if you were a mom, and I a female, though that's gone
right out the culture now ... We might bond. In the
universe, there are no corners, but – I'll fight mine.' I
strike an attitude: where do I do these brave things?

He stares at me, but there's no intimacy. He says,
'You shouldn't be a romantic about Laika. He had a
private life, you know, and you're outside it.' He
searches his brain, as if he's looking for a gift for me:
'You mustn't think I'm gatekeeper to the universe,
inventor of the cosmic stew,' he says: 'Maybe you've
got it wrong, about the particles. It's not sex, sex isn't
part of it, their inner life: of anything. Things split all
by themselves. You may tweak it all, but what it is, is
just the way it is. Being a trans, if that is what you'd
settle for, a go-between, an in-between – you'd see it
as a kind of counselling, a middle way. But even that –
it's all to do with sex, and I don't see it in you, not at
all.'

'There's power, there's money,' I say, boldly.
'Where my folks came from, that mattered more than
stars.'

'You must interrogate your qualities,' he says.
'The starry heavens?' And he draws the skin of
scrawly math aside: 'Or the world of men in chains.'
He points to the trucks, grinding up the street outside

'I might try music,' I tell him. 'That has something of the nebulae, and the ghosts.'

'In any case,' he says, 'We may not see each other this close to again. But with the quantum – the parting is "farewell". Not goodbye! Nothing is lost, nothing is separate. You might even like the taste of lambs.'

This person, I'm trying to make out with her – I say, 'Science – takes you beyond what you might want to know, and then it isn't always useful.'

There's no reply to that: I press on, 'What you don't know's as much a part of you as what you do.'

'Hey,' she says, 'you're trying to make out, I think. You'll have to wait in line. There's others in the frame. That quantum guy who you frequent – he'll shoot you up, and leave you hanging in the black, between a here and there. Best plant your feet and hope you make some leaves.'

Later, she says, 'You'll have to hurry up.'

I say, 'This is hurry. The more hurried, the more it's intimacy,' but she doesn't follow: 'I'm going back,' I tell her, 'Roots. My native soil.'

We lie here, briefly, after: 'On our table, there used to be a flag,' I say. 'But that was not the language that they spoke. They each spoke a different one, besides, the boundaries always change, and they made a compromise with liturgies. A silly thing to argue over, mother and grandfather. No wedding in between. I've the dialect, a thick one. I hope I can make out with it.'

She's impressed, says, 'Then, there's your politics, so much to understand.' She smiles, perhaps she laughs: 'You tutti-fruttis – always splitting up, always identical, amoebas.'

'I'll roam around,' I say. 'Flexible, and not expecting much. Not romanticising dogs.'

'Don't be glum,' she says. 'Remember – the spaces and the fires are all made out of little spermy things, unstable at first and last, fleeting fairies with a skipping rope.'

'Skipping fairies? The old satyr sold you that?' I ask, amazed.

'It was the nicest thing he said. The rest was claws,' she says.

* * *

The night before I leave, there's this music in an old power-house.

They're caricatures, the musicians, each playing a solo in this great grey space. Grey sludge, turned into energies, sharp, pervasive, by the turbines silent turning far below. Caricatures – there's one, the lips like fillet steaks, Del Monicos: another, his thin pointed breasts overhang his drumstick arms. One has a bamboo cage – it seems, that's his head; there's one, a seal, a slug, a grey roll of flesh, another, tiny one, like an insect, red and black, but vigorous, a clarino trumpet – each respectful of the others, blowing, bowing, only when it is their turn. But not like us; we are all much the same, producing different sounds from similar shapes. In this concert each musician is exactly whittled, architectured for the instrument. The instrument's the player – the sound uniquely his. Not the sound you might think we, at our utmost, might make – phrases mimicking the sounds you hear in forests without birds, oceans with no fish, no gulls. Here, there's activity: with spades, with metals upon metals crying, long empty treetrunks blown, or holes with colonies of busy things.

It makes you want to up, and do unthought of acts.

A rusty boat takes you to the island, and my old friends. Daria meets me, 'Once a life they do this dance with swords. Only this day.'

'They do it every night. Last year too,' I say.

'I want Jim to write a sex play,' she goes on. 'Not just for the money, but to celebrate.'

'I thought he did mathematics only?' I say.

'Oh, that was just at school,' she says wildly, air-stroking the buttocks of some shepherds loafing beneath a tree. 'You'd not believe the games we play,' she says, laughing and skipping: 'The climate here, well, it screws you up and blasts you off.'

It's all quite strange with them, another dance with swords. Jim, thin in the head and bloated down below, greets me, mundanely. No athlete, I should say, sexually.

'The house,' says Daria. 'There's a problem with our house. We rented this other one. There's no water here, we find, and it's us who have the bed. But it's adventure for you!'

I ask Jim what he's doing: 'Looking for the proof,' he says. 'It could take fifty years: and then celebrity. If meantime someone else ...'

'And the cheese you make?' I ask.

'Very salty. Even for our taste. You'll try some. We throw lots away. It's unsaleable,' he says.

'Well, there's the dance,' I say to Daria.

'They used to hate the Turks,' she says. 'The Turks kept ships here. Now they're back investing.'

Would she tempt me? I wonder. A garden, at midnight. Make it a hot holiday, then I'd renounce, for loyalty to Jim. No harm done, and, anyway, all this sex business, the talk, turns you off it. Daria gives no sign of wanting anything from me, and I have never fancied her.

I say, 'There's trouble here, it seems. The mainland ...'

'Oh,' says Daria, 'murders, massacres. They're all different, of course. You're supposed to think that. The pattern is the same.'

'Patterns appear in anything,' I say. 'Even a small persecution is something to reflect upon.'

'You mean your small one, you think, that justifies your sulks,' Daria says, and laughs.

'I wish I had the spirit, of those guys who came out of Africa. Our friends, when we were younger. They were revolutionaries, not just dissidents. They had iron inside,' I say.

'You're solemn enough now,' says Daria. 'I expect it's the news about the house. You'll get a wash before you leave, I promise.'

I'm provoked. I wish I'd stayed away. She goes on, 'Remember, I was there too. We cosseted those guys. Armed struggle! That was it. And the privileged ones, we knew them too, how they tried to seem like us, like everyone. But they lived in crap.'

'Yes,' I say, 'Jim was there too. Arguing and nodding.'

'Jim's moved right along,' says Daria.

The knights put on their sword fight. They're quite old men, prancing round and clashing weapons. In miniskirts and waistcoats. I soon wish Suleiman had won the skirmish long ago. Daria's thigh is pressed on mine, then I see it's pressed on Jim's as well – there's more flesh there than when we had been friends. I think of her, heated up, unrobing landscapes of it, flesh unwanted, then unloved.

The night's been hot. There's stinging things. The house is poor. To exit by the door, I'd need to pass through Daria's room. I jump out the window; then I find the bar is closed. Here comes self-pity, I'm the ugly duckling who's become an ugly duck. Too salty, and unsaleable.

When the bar opens, I say, 'A large raki. And I'll just ask for one of your cigarettes.' The guy is sullen, doesn't like 'raki', puts me in a wrong community, the wrong stretch of history too.

Later, I ask Jim, 'What's wrong with your house?'

'It's heirs,' he says. 'Most people here are heirs. Our lawyer too. You need consent. It's all a paper warren. We missed some burrows, so they say.'

The plot behind the rented house is full of staring heirs.

Daria says, 'You're company, of course – but we invited you as well because – you were more militant than us. More active, like. A bigger voice at least.'

I say, 'For people here – you are their bank. You need a lot of cash. And what you take, they'll never get it back.'

'It's Jim,' says Daria. 'He stands upon the law.'

'You're stuck with someone English, Daria,' I say. 'American or suchlike. Find a solution, then he'll think he's won.'

We have the meeting, and it takes me a lot of shouting, but in the end, Jim will pay up. 'I hate this place,' he says.

'Maybe you should join the sword dance,' I tell him. 'Now you know what that's about.'

Later, the bar guy says, 'Yes?'

'More raki, and a shower,' I say. 'And five per cent. The law says I'm a mediator.'

That's done.

'How can we thank you?' Daria asks.

I say, 'Serve the people – that was what they said. Now, you're the people. This is how it's done.'

A year passes. They've moved inland, my friends, and settled firm. Now, it's like a royal court, a stage – we're always on display, or else we overhear.

Here's Daria. I'm carrying a book. It's to start off conversation in a bar. I say,

'Daria, it's about the good. How to want it, how to choose it.'

'It's a small book for all that,' she says.

'Obviously, money is good. It empowers choice,' I say. 'But at this moment – I'm casting off my drizzly pacifism. If there's a good war, I should say, "resist". And "here's my blood".'

'When do you leave?' she asks, 'I've things to say.'

Jim has been ditched, I see. A shadowy figure, with dark wings. I say, 'Jim reminded me of war-debt, hanging there, quite irreversible, never paid off. I guess, Daria, you have had a spree. Shepherds, perhaps. It didn't matter, but it seems it did.'

'Exactly so,' she says. 'But – I never chose Jim. Not as such – I chose companionship. The trouble was the specific; Jim turned out to be a pain.'

'As for war, Daria,' I say, 'I'm waiting for the right one to come along. I'm saving up for stuff you need in fighting – cotton shirts, smart boots – so don't ask me for cash. That's my specific too.'

'Don't try to be a victim, dear,' she says. 'You're quite a strange one, you know, and irreplaceable.'

'And don't turn it round on me,' I say. 'It's money that you need, not me.'

Some things are hard to choose about – countries: for, against; the odd things people believe, that give them heart to put them on the side you back. Well, with these hard things, it's not choice in general that is difficult, it's having any relevance if you choose or don't. The rest, the personal stuff, is easy: drink or sex, or stealing. Do it, or not, according to the little driver, squirming just beneath your hair.

'You're at home here,' Daria says, as I order a nest of sausage.

'Not really. I speak a southern dialect. They rather despise it here.'

'It's a cheap city, in the centre,' she says. 'Your pad – private or public?'

'I don't know,' I say. 'A guy comes round, collecting. Eventually they'll send the cops to throw us out. There's us poor, and there's rich. Markets for us, boutiques for them. No middle. No workers that you see. Those little telephone things that everybody has – they seem to even it all out. Crowds without power, you know, dancing in the streets. It keeps cracking but it goes on. Goes on, slowly down, with dancing. You were the last colonials. It went bad for you. All for money, and nothing commercial. How could that work?'

'Jim's furious. I took his cash. Under the law,' she says.

We go back to my room. I hope Daria doesn't want me to screw her – a reward for the money I won't give her, or a service that I'd owe her for?

'This is a small room,' she says.

'I'm glad you noticed that at once. Some rooms have no quality at all. One of them this room has, yes, it's smallness,' I say.

'Power, evil, violence,' she reads off files. There's not much else. 'It starts with those,' she says, flicking with her nails, 'And ends up somewhere else ... Perhaps. We hope.'

'No, no,' I say. 'I love them. They're the solid things we know about. The trouble is – dilution and dispersion. There's many devils now, each one with a specialisation. No big chief. Lots of powerful men and women, cancelling each other out, or trying to. Violence – well, anyone can do it, it comes naturally to most. The real thing, the solid, essence – it tends to melt away. We see it, think about it – then it slinks off, into the wings.'

She doesn't understand. 'What do you want?' she asks. 'You plan to represent all this? Music, some chords? A picture? Book? Or some of each.'

'Ah yes,' I say. 'That "some of each" ... You've lost the scent. It's dropped into your senses. Who cares if you're a little devil, or you run some office, or a jail? No, I don't like any of these ways, to represent, to cut things into cubes. The book, for instance – it's shut and silent on your shelf. The chord – off it vibes to some black hole. It's changed the thing it represents, it has become a lesser – no, an other – thing.'

'Well,' she says, 'that's just the way.'

'It is, it is,' I say. 'I fear it's so. Those files – those things that's all around, bad things that people say they hate, at least distrust – they treat them like people treat their rats. Ugh – let's get rid of them. Bad things! The answer is – a cat! Or poison. Watch it though! The remedy is worse than the ill. The remedy *is* the ill, in fact.'

'It sounds ambitious,' Daria says. 'As you're not really trained for it. What's in the files? Anything?'

'They're just conversation points. What would yours be called, Daria – love, disappointment, revenge? Sweet, sour, and pickles?'

'It's you who's the reactionary,' she says.

'Yes, it sounds like that,' I say. 'I'm trying to go beyond.'

We crouch down, look out my window: 'I'm on the edge, where those foundering empires scraped together,' I say. 'The ochre one, the blue-green one. Sank, left the hatred bobbing there among the sharks.'

'Well,' says Daria briskly. 'It seems the citizens must all buy vegetables together. By the way, I'm with a guy. You can relax. He has a sister, if it's trouble that you really want. And remember, you're so glib. Real guys are different, they resist. No one's after your ideas, your land, your sacred world. You're just a poor guy, looking on, while real people sweat in their armour, fall dead upon the sands.'

Here's the sister – half-sister maybe – of Daria's boyfriend. Is it a concert, that we're at? It's called 'The Bad Tower'. Maybe after the ones that fell in America. It's not a tower here, it's a heap of bread-coloured bricks, that tumbled when a shell hit somewhere far above, so there's splintery black wood too, fallen from a roof. A guy playing on a single string. He's Vietnamese, it seems.

The sister, Anna, says, 'Why Vietnam? We've lots of martyrs too.' To me, that's too severe.

The string's one note is charged electrically, it shimmers like a patch of oil on water. He doesn't change the pitch, just the intensity, the strength, the timbre. It goes on for as long as you would do yourself – buried under the bricks. Waiting for a siren. Someone coming to rescue, or to finish you off. The crushed chest wearing you out; then through the door, into the white.

'It's electric,' Anna whispers. I don't bother to answer.

'It must be to do with what comes next. More evil. Or – the same. Or something different,' she whispers on.

'It's not knowing where the evil lies,' I say. 'The intention, the collapse? Something conventional we're supposed to know about. Guys doing what they do, aiming their weapons well or badly.'

'It's like a string quartet,' she says. 'While it goes on, you think of something else, or lots of things.'

'I think you must be right,' I say. 'We're being sucked into other people's minds. It's not at all enlightening.'

'The tower above,' she says, 'has disappeared. I guess it was a treasury, a garrison. And down here, a jail.'

I say, 'It's quite as I have said. The bad replaced by bad, by means of badness.'

'We're not the bad ones, anyway,' Anna says, 'not yet, at least. Or not this time.'

'I'll find a situation where that's relevant, and then take sides,' I say.

'Forget it,' Anna says. 'You're a lucky one. Born with nothing, no name, nothing. No clan, no truth. Rejoice. You see us here, stumbling along, trying to toss our burdens in the ditch. We get to do bad things, but underneath it's nothing you'd call bad, only history, and guys who follow you, and pick your burden up, and nail it on your back. Don't meddle. All this stuff about the good – it doesn't enter. We're condemned from birth until we throw our thick selves off, enter the world of ghosts, like you.'

Hats or caps, blues or greens – sides you could choose.

She goes on, 'With you, it's all negotiable. No natural starts and ends. Your philosophers – always indeterminate. Critical of this and that, or lessons wrongly learned. It's slip and mud. You try to sound decisive, but it's bullfrogging. Arp, arp, you cry.'

'Maybe I'd like to be something, by birth,' I say. I'm not convinced.

'Forget your questioning,' she says. 'Being involved with me – your bones will burn within. Doubt's your vocation, stay with it. I'd take no gift from you. You take them back.'

She's running far ahead. I don't much like her. Gifts are not proposed, are not in prospect.

'I told you,' Daria says. 'Anna is angry. If that's what it is. Funny family – I'm with Omar, as you know. The brother – he is angry too – with Jim, with me. Anger's my destiny, it seems.'

'I'll dump those files, I think,' I say.

'Well, it's a start,' says Daria. 'But it doesn't lead you on to somewhere else. You can't go to concerts all your life. Or shows.'

'Omar's a bandit,' Anna says. 'We'll see his territory.'

'What does he want with Daria?' I ask.

'Not concerts. Money, I expect,' she says.

We take two horses: 'Nothing special about these?' I ask. Just brown. Anna doesn't answer.

Up to the forest skirt. The pines stand on each others' knees, looking upwards. Logs lying idle.

'The people here went off,' says Anna. 'Some went to Canada, or the like. Mine too. They're ghosts. Over there, even their Indians are ghosts.'

It was always difficult, here. And cold. People eked out. Down in the valley, squeezing motorcars into sprints of road, lots of people, walking.

The horses know their job. They climb up and down. We see the backsides of big animals, departing through the trees. It's not at all like movies. Here's Omar.

I ask him, 'Do you hunt the animals?'

He says, 'Of course not. We're the last free people here. They're free too, they eat each other, like they have to do. We don't interfere.'

'Where's all the other guys?' asks Anna.

'Oh, they're up and down,' says Omar: he has a four-part tic, he has to do it all, each time, his face a tape-loop. 'No one's after us,' he says. 'So why bunch all together?'

Omar goes through his tic, over and over. You have to look away. It's like Anna says, a string quartet. I can't, prefer not to, imagine what trauma set it up. An execution threatened? One he's done? You have to get inside his head:

Omar thinks, *There's nowhere else to go. The trees, that never lose their leaves, the animals, they hunker down, there's snow, and there they are again, rejuvenated, learning the world again, in spring. It's better than the factory, so long as no one comes ...*

Again the tic – you and he must go all through it, or who knows...? Humans are the only animals who don't know what's in their neighbour's head. So they must guess:

Daria: she thinks – *I screwed up, but I've done no bad. I've landed up quite wonderful, in fact. It's tough here, but it's tougher still if you belong – and that tic, it's on my nerves, but not so heavily as being with an English guy ...*

Daria's an opportunist, Anna thinks. *She's lucky to have opportunities. Surely, no one thinks her problems are equivalent to ours? It's just about her choice....*

That's what is good about Daria, Omar thinks. *She hasn't fallen down. Here, everything has fallen down. Now, what we do, we do in self-defence, not good or bad.*

Aloud, I ask Anna, 'Does Omar really have all those comrades? And all on horses?'

'Oh yes,' she says. 'You think it's all a joke? Some things, if you write them down, they seem exaggerated, quite overdone. But no, he is exactly what he says.'

'Maybe we should make a house for him,' I say.

I think of blue-green stone, some fluting, stucco perhaps, carvings in fine woods.

We pile some logs – the vertical's forsaken, down they lie. We make a tent-shape with some sticks, quite low it sits, and cover it with sheets of tin. A bandit's lair. Here, he could watch the wolves and foxes, imagine elephants, the mushrooms red upon the ground and green on trees, no pines but foliage, medicinal and rare ...

'You can't expect I'd spend some time in this,' says Omar, irritated. 'What'd I eat?'

'Omelettes at Daria's, like you always do,' says Anna, quite put out. 'You can lie here, it's a therapy for what you've got.'

We ride back to the city. We hand the horses in, and they don't look back at us. Anna says, 'You can boil water many times. Over and over. Just the same heat each time, or even less. All those Greeks are dead, who thought everything was the first time and nevermore. If we had positions, officially, we could make a noise – inside. Not in the street, throwing stuff and daubing columns, but saying things worth enough to print on paper. All is travelled over – many of the best parts have been dug up, or melt. We're all bandits, in our dens. No one looks for us, and we rob modestly.'

I say, 'Anna, you're a ticket-seller. That's cultural production.' She's angry,

'Me being ordinary and having fixed ideas – gives you no rights at all on me. Even to talk about me.'

Later, I say to Daria, 'Anna, Omar – they must have some history about them.'

Daria says, 'Things like war – they fly over almost all of us, a big bird, like an eclipse. There's happy survivors, and sad ones. Anna isn't one or other. Just neutral – and what's come after, to her it seems a picture with the interesting things left out. Nothing is resolved, everything is changed. Omar feels it should go on, to some resolution, some answer. But of course, it isn't so. At least there's nothing drastic. Not for him, at least.'

'Things like war,' I say. 'The history they've survived, Omar and Anna, is things like economics too: and neighbours. The war consumed them both, but lots of stuff was left, to be lived through. Well, we're all neighbours, I guess, of different sorts. It's like me knowing all the people that I know because they're friends of someone else.'

'Don't push the neighbours thing,' says Daria. 'You live in a place, so you must have neighbours too. I didn't see any. Does that mean you think they won't come after you? You could live in the woods, like Omar. His neighbours are all covered in fur, and they can really be indifferent.'

Later, 'Daria,' I say, 'there is no hurry. The commission owed for settling your dispute back there – I'll just take five per cent. These honourable debts – it's what makes civilisations work.'

She looks away and says, 'We've settled Omar, like Tecumseh. Let's hope he's no ambitions. Better his indelible tic than painting faces, whittling the arrows,' but she pays me, not quite five per cent.

'Jim's after you,' she says, 'He knows you made the bargain for the other side, and took their cash. He thought you were a friend, so now he'll kill you.'

'That's the law,' I say, I'm not concerned. He doesn't speak the language, he does not exist, and I'm protected.

'We're not Indians, though,' says Anna. 'We had no lands, no way of life to lose. Just a before, and then an after.'

Go on, Anna, I think, don't tell me the experiences, I know all about them. Terrible. The courage – yours. The cowardice – hypothetically mine. That becomes the empathy you grieving storytellers need. The suffering. It's all a story now. It passed through you skewering like a steel, and now there's nothing left of you. That's why you're angry. Daria's more a real person, whole, if dented.

'You can be so arrogant because nothing ever happened to you,' Anna says.

Anna's room is hung with red and green. Like the mushrooms. You don't ask where all the relatives have gone. The cloths and cushions – they smell like in the tourist shop – your bus stops ten minutes, and you buy the first things. They don't fit anywhere.

'It's all consequences,' Anna says. 'What goes on, it all depends on what you did before. Mistakes mature, they're never solved. You have your revolution, but you have to keep on killing oppositions. Then you kill your friends. And you're left with crap, and executioners. You make a country, but it turns out a box of toys, the soldiers eat the bears and blow the trumpets. It never ends, on and on,' and I say, to keep her quiet, 'A tic?'

'You think it's the same for everyone?' she asks. 'It's even worse for some, because you can't submit, squat low enough. The others want your feathers and your song.'

'You ask the hard questions, Anna,' I say. 'Though they've all turned into pop.'

'All those dead people that we never knew,' she presses on. 'Making things unsolvable for us. So ignorant ... and we're supposed to study them!'

In the red and green, she's a drab defiant bird, with polished eyes, beak a bit askew. This place is right – for colour, for her. No chicks. Nothing belongs to her, if it ever did. Omar balances her – his tepee is all his, or lifted off from stacks of logs cut for no fires.

'You care, you calculate,' says Anna. 'Just for yourself. But people out to get you – they don't care at all. They calculate so as not to have to care.'

'Everyone ends up in the way they most have feared,' says Daria. 'What am I doing here? Omar's like a mole, marooned above ground, his claws blunted, no penetration, can't shrug himself through the topsoil. Can't get down to all kinds of other people that we can't imagine, underground.'

'Anna thought the worst,' I say. 'That didn't happen. Other things instead. Perhaps it's wait and see.'

'For me,' says Daria, 'down on the river's sandy shore. The sword, the lance, into my mouth, and down my throat, down, down, the blood a spring stream pouring up, the steel going down, and never finishing. That, I can feel.'

'It has to be a warrior does that,' I say. 'That isn't Jim. The only warrior round here is me, and I'm undecided. The others, soldiers, neighbours, the militias – they were scum with swords – or something like.'

'They always are,' says Daria, cresting on her myth. 'It's what they say they want that counts. That makes the sound, brings the public in. That awful death – it's not a thing I want – but it's the picture that I've carried round ...'

'Is it regret, or guilt?' I ask. 'Daria, you know – the point is not the diet and the prayer, it's finishing the longest journey you can make,' and I don't say, 'Without your hamstrings being cut,' for Daria has risked exactly that.

'Oh no,' she says, 'I know it's not about the temples other people want to build. It's – not falling off the path when you are in the gang; and the marble block you're carrying not smashing you.'

I tell all this to Anna. It seems to justify my being here. Observing for some purpose. She says,

'You guys all justify yourselves. Because you think you have survived, and there's some merit gained.' She stands, and lifts one foot, a hand tight holds it behind her thigh. It's quite remarkable.

I ask, 'Are they temples, Anna, that they say they want to build? Are there gods we must believe in?'

'It's always self-defence,' she says. 'Everything. Always, and nothing more.'

'We understand each other, Anna,' I say. 'The history you've seen, shooting quills like porcupines. And yet it's Daria I can chat to. She only wants to be a tragedy, it's quite pathetic. Like Narcissus.'

Anna says, 'It's not true, about the porcupines. They only threaten, standing there. If Daria can't believe in anything except her destiny, maybe she'd prefer to end up as a cult. Me – I hope my story's over.'

We're all there – Omar too. And Jim. Omar says, 'My horse needs watering.'

We're by the river. There's the spit of sand. Has Daria's moment come, I wonder – no, Jim's not a warrior, nor an athlete. He'll not assassinate, nor run.

Jim squares up to me, and says at last he's found me. That is true. There's shouting, in two languages at least – that's my defence, to hide behind my dialect. He waves small fists. He doesn't understand the law, and its financial gaze. 'And in cahoots with Daria there,' he shouts, 'to rob me of the future I'd prepared.'

There's insults now for Daria. It's not a classic speech – the theme is cash, some sex as well.

We all step back. He has his stage. The only one he doesn't hate is Anna. I'm alarmed for her. The story often ends with slaughtering the innocents. But not this time.

Omar is watering his horse, and going through his tic, and Jim – maybe he pushes Omar. When they show the film, the frame where all the action fits is always cloudy, or has been snipped right out. So, suddenly, there's Jim, he's on his knees, a steel is in his throat, the blood ...

'Oh no,' shouts Daria, 'the idiot! He's done for Jim! That pointed thing – it's not a sword – maybe some kitchen tool, a ladle, or the thing they hang stuff from ...'

She's very analytical. We bury Jim, in silence. We maybe should have thought of something else, but at the time, it seemed the best, the only ritual. Omar is silent too, having seen this all before, in war, from many sides.

'It's a mistaken subject we have here, a wrong case,' Daria says at last. 'A hunting accident. The unarmed one got killed. The hunt is made of that. The prey – is usually unknown until it's in the bag,' but we are silent for a while, for Jim – so charged with bile and words, and accusations, mostly true – is suddenly reversed. Becoming silent, undisturbed.

DOWN FROM THE STARS

'I told you so,' says Anna, 'It's always self-defence.'

'It might be one of Omar's brigands did it, unexpectedly,' I say: 'They'll hunt for him. We're Omar's alibi,' though I'm the only one who has no interest at all in Omar's fate. The others know. They stare at me. I am the heir of secrets unconfessable. 'I'm with you guys,' I say.

'Any of us,' says Omar. 'We could have done it – but the guy, Jim, was poor, a foreigner. What could he expect? You go into the forest – there it's full of strange and venerable things. The huts, the trees, the bears, the axes and the woodsmen – my! what a story there. It's a whole history. Poetic too – the spit of sand, the spit of blood – that can't avail, of course, and slaughter with a piece of spit from someone's chimney, where they smoked bears' paws and turkeys too ...'

We put Jim beneath the sand. The river will wash him. 'Sand to sand,' says Anna.

'Should we have said something?' Daria asks. 'I used to know a bit of Kaddish,' though it seems she has forgotten, when she tries.

'Was he devout?' I ask, 'Although the prayer might be for us.'

'Jim believed in retribution, punishment,' says Omar. 'And he got a lot of that. Law too. You can't

insult the people. Look at my brothers, over there –
fighting the lawlessness, imprisonment, bombard-
ments, torture. Things that can't endure.'

Anna says, 'Trouble he sought, trouble he got.
The lessons end right there.'

We stand around, our hands and arms raised, or
folded, in the prayer – that we not be found out; as
guilty, of just being there, or muddling the rituals.

'If he'd been a hero,' Omar says, 'you'd need a
guslar. But not this case, for jealousy and cash –
besides, he wasn't worth a ...' We hope he doesn't say
'a spit'. Instead, he pauses, then he says 'a nickel'.

'What will become of Omar?' Anna asks: 'Where can
we send him?'

'Oh no,' says Daria, 'the poor guy's unemployed.
And I love him so – let him stay up there, up in his
wood.'

'Is he religious? Or a democrat?' I ask. 'We could
send him East.'

'Look,' Omar says, 'come on guys! I'm still here.
I've done my stint. More, in Jim's case. Just leave me
be. There's cash behind it all, the banks, the East ... I
want no part in that.'

We stand, we look, we've had our say. Behind most things, there are Americans, we know.

'They make them take an oath, the guys like Jim,' says Anna. 'It's with them till they die.'

'Dear Jim,' says Daria. 'He was so much more than oaths – the math, the proof in fifty years, and that unwritten play.'

We talk of Omar's destiny. We must fit in the foreigner, unknown, slaughtered on the shore, by chance. The offer of a voyage, it should have been. Leaving the beloved. Great things done, return in triumph after tribulation.

'No, no,' says Omar. 'I'll not go. No epics, no monkey armies. I'm quite happy, hidden here. Jim struck me – you all saw ...'

And as he talks, it seems to us Jim did, or something like.

'All right,' says Daria, 'Omar stays with me. It's not a holy war I have to offer, nor democracy. Complicity in silence – that's the best life has in store for him. Holy war? Voting and parliaments – it's quite grotesque, for him, or any of us. He doesn't want the risk, either. No, you must help us,' and she puts her paws around me. 'You can take Anna, if you want.'

Anna's not keen: she says to me, 'It's true there's not much for you here. At least – you make nothing happen.'

'What do you propose?' I ask.

Daria is eager: 'You go back there, and you be Jim. There, no one knows you – no one will suspect that Jim lies here beneath the sand. With all the others.'

I say, 'There is a flaw. No one knows Jim here, or they don't care. There, it's true, I'm quite unknown. But "there" – is where they knew quite well what Jim was like, his features, why he left. All that.'

'You'd need to take good care about the details,' Anna says.

'What was Jim in?' I ask.

'Oh – oil and banks, and government, and military stuff,' says Daria. 'And people move around. One Jim is like another. Sort it out.'

I'm quite intrigued. And Daria says, 'You do it, and I'll pay.'

'Let's go in here,' says Juan, a Mexican. 'My feet are tired.'

It's not a movie, it's a kind of show. There's jugglers, dwarves – not so called, of course – sword swallowers. Better trained than Jim. And some big poppy, President, some guy says.

Yes, here he is. The chief.

'I've always been a communist,' says the President. 'They can't impeach me, as it's not a crime. It doesn't make much difference, of course, because unlike you idiots,' and he waves over the inattentive crowd, 'I study history. Now is not the time, and not the country. You guys out there, you have a little way to run. Your revolutionary impulse, well, it's winding down, and when it sputters out, you'll step aside, others will be found ...'

There's cheers. My new friend, Juan, says, 'I'd always hoped to hear a speech like that.'

The crowd calms down, and eats its stuff.

'We must be mistaken,' I say.

'Let's go ask him,' says Juan. So, when the show is over, that we do.

'Hey, you guys been drinking?' asks the President. 'Communism? It's true I talk a lot about the working stiffs, and trailer families, and helping out. But that's my job, and how I keep it, too. There's all those guys out there, they come in, they cheer, their feet are tired – and they expect my kind of thing. It's like the Indians, who tell you El Dorado's down the road, quite near. But think! The job is this as well, that I'm a general; then there's the prisons, all those flying

bombs, and seeing military stuff is stored, and the gasoline, and the cash is printed, bundled up. But communism! You are out of date, my friends.' He laughs, and turns away.

'I don't see a contradiction there,' declares my friend, 'except it's maybe by some other names.'

I insist, 'Hi! Mr President! I'm Jim. I want to ask – are we headed for extinction, do you think? The species? What's your plan?'

'Hi, Jim!' he says. 'What you got for me? Money for my campaign? Advice? Well, anyway – some things happen, some things may happen, or are destined one day to happen. I do what I can, that is the job. You can't just do what everybody wants.'

'Jim wasn't like that at all, my Jim,' says Daria, crossly. 'He wasn't an idiot, if that's what you mean.'

'You see!' I say, 'I said it wouldn't work. No, no, I won't go.'

'This Juan,' Anna asks. 'What is he? An avatar?'

'He doesn't exist,' I say. 'I'd like to have a friend, met quite casually, on the bus – after the

disappointment come the lies, the cover-ups. History –
those writers! Then, everyone looking back, inventing,
tradition, home-cooking, tasty snacks, that crap.'

'You shouldn't have expected more,' Anna says.
'You'd know, if you'd suffered. And people look back
because they made the wrong turn.'

'I don't need suffering to know,' I say. 'And they
look back because there's no way forward. They're not
looking for a better path – they want a place to sit
down and stay.'

'If there's no rain, no fire, Omar's at peace,' says
Anna.

'Anna,' I ask. 'What was the terrible thing for
you?'

'Nothing. The fear. I was too young. The fear
stays all your life. Corrodes.'

'That's all?' I ask again. 'And Omar?'

'Just stories. They were quite enough.'

'Enough of this old harrowing stuff,' says Daria.
'It passes over everywhere. Now, it's passed ...' She
brightens up. 'I'm thinking – I may run.'

'Running's always good,' says Anna. 'Maybe you
should wait until the threat ...'

'No, no,' shouts Daria. 'Running for election. And
the threat – is me!'

I think, I couldn't stop anything. That's the logic
of it – when it happens, you can't intervene, past or

future, and I say, 'Daria, you represent no one, not even you.'

'Forget the representation bit,' she says. 'It's more persuasion, making a figure, having it catch on. I'll learn the language properly, make some friends. Elsewhere, the army and the gangs are separate. Here, it's all the same, the cops, the smugglers, politicians – it's quite renaissance, everyone fights all the rest, the result is, it makes a splendid show ...'

We can't imagine what to say. She says, 'I want to be great. A prince. An infinity greater than Jim, with his jobs, his state, the things he wouldn't do. Omar will sit – not at my right hand – just sit. Lots did it so, like me – the foreigner who dominates.'

The world is full of it – the ambition. I say to Anna, 'I guess Daria is real – but now, I'm interested in an ideal love that doesn't leave me, and of course I can't get near ... It seems it's not the stars. Maybe it's contraband, maybe it's you, though I'm not sure ...'

Anna's interested, for once. 'You could build a Taj Mahal. Or, better, Daria can. Is your lover to be male or female?'

'How can you tell?' I say. 'They are imaginary.'

Daria romances on about herself. 'It's much more than power – the Prince, that guy, how dull, just doing down and keeping on. I want splendour. Bringing people in, having them make things, adorn the streets –

all people from the East. Even an atom bomb – no, not to drop, where's the fun there. No, to play the game, and fire guys up.'

I say, 'It all seems in the past. Being grandiose, all that. And the cash is dirty – they'll catch you for that.'

'No,' says Daria. 'I'm not into grubby stuff. Guys here don't like paying taxes – so meantime, I'd take it from the gangs. And concerts – lots of those. Festivals too.'

'I'm not so fearful now,' says Anna. 'It's something else, you slip it under all my skins. In like a needle ... Not hunting me, just gangster stuff. Anything for Omar – he'll be the grumpy consort for anyone.' She's converted. It was quick.

'Anna,' says Daria, 'I could bring you out. Staying close, but also friends with corrupt, shifty guys, having a laugh, some fun as well.'

'No, Daria, you can't,' I say. 'That's poncing,' and she says,

'You foolish man! If I go down, no harm will come to her. This is new life. Besides, you never wanted her?'

'Well, no,' I say, and Anna says, 'Yes. I should like that. That is me. Let's do that. Yes, yes. Some life!'

I go on. I feel I must, I say, 'And all the problems here. Beliefs and none, the musics various, the jailers and the jailed rotate like spinning coins ...'

'Of course,' says Daria. 'And you can bet – I shan't do anything at all about that. What do you expect? I'm not in that line at all, and you're a fool to think than anybody steps right in and steps right out again, doling out some medicine. The problems – let them think things for themselves.'

Later, Omar asks me, 'What can I do with this crazy woman?'

'Slump malignly on your throne,' I say. 'There's Darias all round, they're dumped, and then they want to rule. They climb some ways up on the hill – and then, if they don't fall, they stick.'

Omar says to me, 'Anna – she's always wanted that, to be a courtesan. It was her aim, until the fear took hold.' There's nothing I can say. We're at a concert, Anna's wearing furs, that maybe Omar caught. Daria's there too, proud, her age spots decked with rubies. Omar tags along.

On the stage, there's dancers, pink and blue, they run from side to side, some as if they've leaden butts, and others striving tall as feathers. Then, they toss each other against wires, some huge machine back there – is it a harp? An egg-slicer, for monstrous eggs? The sound is quite aeolian, I think. Oh, what a bore. To stay here, probably for years, and see them truck in stuff like this ... the vital charge runs down, and Daria – she'll rise.

Afterwards, she stands there, cloak round Anna, Omar. A queen, two knaves. Oh Anna, I think, I'm so sorry, so sorry, I'd got your destiny all wrong.

I leave, I need to take a break. I hitch a ride. Some guys are packing boxes on the truck – full of skulls, all measured long ago, and classified – by religion, community, and maybe other things as well. The families, all jumbled up. Some with no relatives; and I think – there lies Jim, buried, waiting for discovery and being classified.

'Who's the fat dame waving?' asks the driver-soldier.

Daria wants to make sure I'm off. This trip – I've done it many times, always come back. I say,

'She's big mass, in the culture. Brings the money in, the liberals as well. Respectable – that's the aim. Some bosses who can sing, they say it softens everything.'

He doesn't speak. I say,

'They do the sword dance twice a day. They've lightened up, there's girls.'

He's silent.

'What's the skulls for?' I ask.

A pause, then he says, 'We've bodies that might fit. They'll be re-classified, at all events.'

Casually, I ask, 'Anyone from the river?'

'Oh,' he says, 'I just ferry them. Not their past or future, nor how they've ended up.'

'Well,' I say, 'what luck I came across you,' and he makes sounds with his nose. He doesn't take my tip.

Then, I take the train. This new city doesn't suit. Some concerts, but more demos, cheaper; greater thresh of bodies, vague hopes carried off in vans. I couldn't tolerate restraint, hands tied, and left face down. Sit-ins folding you in tiny spaces – best to hover near the back and stretch your legs, in running, too. Always there's some guy who says, 'Forget the victims, they've been wasted, or they're turned towards vague hopes. What you need's the revolutionary core.'

The vanguard. It's not here. Vienna, Moscow.

Political freedom in the little things. No work. Maybe I don't know what to do with bigness, littleness ... or work.

Here's the train station, open all the time. The only place to shop. What a bordello! The Trans-

Siberian Railway – there go the trans! – and after, Siberia, trans guys looking at life from both sides or more, each shackled to their privates – then we'd reach Japan, America. Geishas with pink hair. Pretend geishas with real pink hair ... Some acid trip – the faint blue nightlights, samovars and samoyeds, and sex. What else is there to do? – the taiga, mammoth tusks like sabres drawn – a million of them. Jim's Indiana bones.

I take another train, go back down to Daria, home. Here's Anna, pearls clasped around her neck, quite beautiful, now she's set her price. A choker – river pearls, no doubt.

'How's the scene up there?' Daria asks me.

'The avant garde? It's not there. Just guys who've lucked with impresarios. News from the river here?' I ask.

She says, 'Jim has company. Some guys that didn't recognise their breaks. Some take their liberties, and some get charred. We could find Jim, disperse him. For a mathman, it would delight. The pieces disassembled all. I found his menu card – the CIA canteen. The chip is live.'

'An emergency ration,' I say, but she is not amused: 'They've stuff from everywhere, and fresh each hour,' she says. 'There's swedes, blue anchovies, and puffing fish. Goat's humbles in a pie, and karakorum sheep, and Colonel Pepper's stick. There's aloe sauce with coca on the side, and monkey's lobes in ale ...' She's memorised it all, and then disguised it like a chef would do.

* * *

'This new art, it's heavy stuff,' says Daria. Crates of it, from trucks. She goes on, 'After bourgeois art – here it comes, more bourgeois art. Where's the new? I ask. I can't conceive ... It's already all been covered. Next, there comes world's end. And roll up, crowds – you ought to see that too, it's quite unmissable.'

It's brave stuff that she talks – it could bear a religious twist, quite messianic. But she's really interested in other things. Offload the sculptures – then in go other boxes, ours, untaxed, and even heavier, going north.

Omar stands round, he's hung with silver chains, he has a platinum quiff. Not much for him to do. He's cosy in his niche. I ask,

'Where did your unit go?'

'Oh,' he says, 'a factory opened, then it closed. That was the rhythm that they had to dance to – not quite an insult ... lowering, that's it. Me – I'm into trees – the lovely ones, quite tall, unsuitable for timber, though. And in my head. Groves, gardens – that's what I need. I mean, that's what we need.'

'I love your mèche, Omar,' Daria tells him, meaning she doesn't. 'Guys here – you're a bouquet of thistles, that's how you hang together. Get out of it, my dear – join a fanclub, football or music, it's all the same. It wears me down, you, Omar ... then there's Anna, with her, it's all about men, but not with sex. Luring generals into her tent and cutting off their heads. Except she doesn't have a knife, and there she is at dawn, some louche guy crawls out from her lair, and there she is again, her *smorfia*, contempt at who knows who and probably at everyone ...' She talks on, and on. I feel I'd like to meet some real tough people, not clowns like these, slipping on blood and doing pratfalls.

Anna says what luck – the war here wasn't rockets, stuff passing overhead unseen, with projects talked about round tables – but neighbours. Fighting. Eyeing your goats and chickens.

'The next one will be big enough,' I say. 'All passing overhead. There's no one coveting your rocks. Next time, you'll be the lucky ones.'

Still, we're all waiting.

'Silly boy,' says Daria. 'Look at us all here, survived. Besides, war is just a poker game. There's

famine, epidemics, falling in the street, not waking up
...'

'All those you can make bets against,' I say. 'I
agree with you, for sure – it's just this place makes you
think of buildings falling down, and guys with
billhooks at your door.'

'Maybe there's an earthquake, and they've come
to dig you out,' she says, dismissively. 'It's all just
pride and prejudice. Those shows are there to make
you think of other things.'

What can Anna do, but seek a sheltering wing? She's
doing well, she glows, she shows her skin, her eyes are
black and hot, they follow promise round the room, as
it drinks champagne and Chivas ... Here's one now – a
youngish guy, not bad, not bad, he's maybe wearing
corsets, or it's just the fashion, the belly rising up
around his breasts. He talks some politics – maybe his
militia's into football, or some other sport, and wins its
medals on the playing field ...

'My hair's so thin,' says Daria, showing a wisp.
Her butcher's arms, crinkly expanses of brown tripe ...
She says to me, 'Find out about Anna's boy. The new
one over there. I fancy him. Don't be afraid – be
discreet instead. They all sneak up on all, vainglorious

guys, they spy each other out. He won't notice you – he'd notice me.'

'If I get threatened, I'll back off,' I say, backing right off.

'Yes, dear, do that,' Daria says, 'and I'll not tell on you, you bet. Everything I know ...'

'Dear child,' Daria says to me, 'you'll write the programme notes – there's some new guys, a Dutch one, and a Russian. Those old ones – they truck round heavy stuff that costs to set it up – photos a metre square, and dolls. Oh, what a bore, their rhapsodies. And porno stuff that comes from cans ...'

I write, 'The canals run to the sea, grey snakes. I'm a punk, I've shaved my hair. Here I sit, upon this wall. Pink flowers like buttons. Maybe it's Delft. Am I a boy, or girl? I've streaked my face. We stride out of this film, those bullies have done awful things to me, but now we're dancing in the wood – there's soldier ants with javelins – a black thing like a turtle, spinning with a bear. The bear puts out his tongue – my, it's so long and red – and we're are back in film again, I'm dancing with the bear, he picks me up, he cradles me, he could be father, mother – then he grasps the zip – off comes his head ...'

'No, no,' shouts Daria, when she sees the writing. 'You haven't even seen the goddam stuff. This rubbish, sentimental, inconsequential crap – and what's this first person ghoul, the ghost that conjures up this yarn and knits it into sacks?'

'The programme's to be printed long before I see the shows,' I say. 'And people like an "I", it humanises, makes it all more real to have a real person, telling all, explaining ...'

'No, no, disaster,' Daria says. 'You haven't got the knack. To write high-fly you must have had a life of flying high.'

This must be Vlad. He's tall and fair: he says, 'Is this the stuff I should have brought? Am I the bear? What fun! I find a building, usually, and do the numbers on it. What are they, numbers? People you'll never see, gone down, or secrets leading out the garden, up the path that leads to fame?'

He ingratiates himself so easy. Here comes Maas – a dirty beetly guy. He says, 'Starts with a punk? Oh yes. That's brilliant. That's the hook that catches whales – the issues, they're like spouts, that people recognise. Everyone that's not at war is hunting whales ... Dancing with bears? Now, that's a thing I never would have thought ...'

They both know I'm a genius. I make their life, and ease it for them.

'It's all business now,' says Maas. 'It doesn't look as if you do much here.'

'This is a transit zone,' I say. 'Some things in passing linger on.'

'I'd rather like to buy some diamonds, with my fee,' says Maas. 'If you have mines, that is.'

'Diamonds we do,' I say. 'The problem is your fee. You have to work for that.'

'I need something too, to take away,' says Vlad. 'My numbers often make some acolytes. God is a prime, you know, immortal, but you can slice some fractions off a prime. That's what you usually see – some place that wallows in neglect, no jobs, no stuff, guys young and ignorant – they're fired up with the truth, some musty fraction ... My numbers – so clean, inedible. And wholesome too.'

'You must know Maas from somewhere else,' I say. 'He's into business too, and fame. I guess they go together, in a modest way.'

'We share a view,' says Vlad. 'We're not afraid of being right.'

I think awhile, and say, 'I accept that I'm a genius. But substituting this for that – numbers for faith ... I'd sooner back away. That's not my path.' Vlad stares at me in admiration, and I think of Jim ... the proof that was to take his lifetime, and instead his life terminated in indifference. Into the river, no one mourned him, his numbers tumbled in the water, a last wriggle like a fly's grub. I say aloud, 'his number's up,' and Vlad lets out a laugh.

Daria's thrilled, the bill is full, almost. 'We play a game,' says Maas. 'We call it justice. Take some names – the public decides, which is worse? Or what's the punishment? Or the reward. Bonaparte or Genghiz Khan. Sinatra-Riefenstahl. You do it all with strings, or buttons. Nothing too complex.'

'It sounds quite vulgar, Maas,' I say.

'No, no, it's silly, it's a circus,' Vlad corrects. 'And what is even more exciting – you can play it with your friends, and on your friends. And raise the stakes – with dead guys, it's quite an academic ploy. With living ones – you make them scamper, justify, and plead.'

'You all make fun of me, as I am ugly, old,' says Daria: no, obviously she doesn't say that, no one ever does. She wants judgement, still digging up her Jim, reburying in sand. I ask her,

'Where did you get these two, these clowns?'

'Mind yourself,' she says. 'A question so may mean you look for judgement for yourself. And – they're not clowns. They were riggers, in the same circus, doing all the work, the wires, the nets. And then the sawdust for the blood. Now, they make the public do the work.'

'What is their goal?' I ask.

'Why, of course – the general will. They vote, the public. They think, react, then vote. Eventually, they'll decide, with one pure voice, refined – this one to the gallows, that to the pyre, the other to the throne-room, that one cased in liquid gold, with emeralds in his ears.'

'So, the project is a long one?' I persist.

'They'll do a tour,' she says. 'It's better than we sit at home, and reason this and that before blank screens.'

'I think it's wonderful,' says Anna suddenly. 'It's about desire, what's left when you've had your presents. And after, when you've screwed the guy who gives you them.'

'Your man must be a pain,' says Daria, with conviction, 'but he's our protection, our blind eye.'

'And the artists – beautiful. Maas in painted stone, quite life-size, and Vlad, in thornwood,' and as she speaks we see them as she does, beautiful, not what they say or do at all.

'It's true,' says Maas, flexing an arm, the other holding in his painful back. 'Vlad's my couple, my completion. Where we differ's just in what we most enjoy. Me – my girl, she's from Japan. I've known her for some months. Eating crayfish with her – what a joy. And Vlad, his bicycle – climbing the mountains, each day a challenge easily faced down ...'

'And that's just our aesthetic side,' says Vlad. 'Desire is something else, comes from you all. All you public.'

'Well, public I have none,' Daria says, hurrying away. 'With Jim, longing was a jar of caramels between us. Each fishing in, and taking out a different taste; but Omar – he's as flat as tin.'

Maas talks about the circus – swinging on the ropes. Bouncing in the net. The chimps. The knives, the fleshy women – bunnygirls in toppers. Vlad nods. Yes, they've rehearsed all this. In circuses, you rehearse all day. Firing each other from the cannon.

'You do it all,' says Maas. 'And sweat. The others just applaud – or think you cheat.'

I think – here, we've had our lives.

Vlad winks at me – 'You must like concerts. In the ring, you hardly hear the music, you're too busy. The music cheers you up, I bet.'

'Oh yes,' I say.

'You understand, we wanted you guys – to do the work. Make judgements, have some fun, and sweat,' says Vlad.

'We'll try it out with Anna, and her guy,' says Maas. Vlad laughs.

'It's not for punishment, you'll see,' says Maas. 'We'd not presume. It's more a prize. Now, hold these ropes, one red, one green. The red for her, the green for him. And when we say to think, and "start", you pull the rope for who you want to win the prize.'

It's good I don't have to decide on punishment. A prize for what, though? Anna gets prizes all the time ... I see Vlad staring at me, little sneery mouth all twisted up in expectation. How do they fix the ropes? Well, all that circus work, and being intellectuals – they must have found some ways.

It's all – too circusy ... Too game show, too much coarse giggling. I pull the red rope, Anna's. A prize, some clowning trickery, perhaps, an improvising on the stage, and all part friends.

'Well, that was brave,' says Maas. 'A punishment for Anna's man, a prize for her. Let's hope he doesn't croak – we'd all be in a mess. That wasn't diplomatic, choosing so – a little moralistic, when we told you that it didn't count. But – courage. You show lots of that.'

'I didn't understand,' I say. 'I chose the easy option, so I thought. The red rope for a prize. Something for her, and not for him. You didn't say that punishment came in, whichever rope I pulled.'

'It always does,' says Vlad. He hugs himself. 'Even clowns know that.'

'What's my prize?' asks Anna. 'It can't be something that I want, or I'd have had it long ago,' and that is almost certainly the case. She's lovely now – you see she's eating well and going late to bed, she's quite desirable; it's going to the market place, it quite transforms, just like they say. Riches and influence light up her face like patchouli, mascari, all the rest ... she's quite unrecognisable, from when she was that sparrowy pecking thing come orphaned from the war.

Omar pushes in, he says, 'I bet it's some critique, that prize. A book; or tokens if they can't decide,' and Anna says, 'Oh no, a book! You're right. I'll never have the time, I never take the train, here there aren't tracks.' She holds the volume up. It's called *A Sentimental Education*, and she says, 'Oh no! It's literature, and probably it's snide as well. It's long, and that is not the only difficulty ...'

We're quite indifferent to that. It's her guy's punishment that resonates. We go to look for him, Omar like a pointer dog runs on ahead, up past the loggers, skirting burnt-out things that might be anything, and then—

'Oh no!' he says. It's Zef. It's Anna's man.

The guy's been nailed up on a tree, just like in movies, though it's rare in life, it being difficult, with not much point, when you are keen to get away. The uniform – 'It's beautiful,' says Omar, pulling off some parts. The guy is all in black, with silver facings, baggy pants, a black moustache stuck on, and pistols dangling from his gut. 'A bandit chief!' says Vlad, with glee, 'and all that with one pull, that red rope doesn't lark around.'

'Vox populi has done for him, and in a classic way,' says Maas, who seems the poet of the two.

'That's terrible,' shouts Omar, 'Now his band will seek revenge, we'll all end up in sand, the river flowing over, bearing off identity, our eyes, our nose,' he holds his face as if erasure's just begun.

'I'll save the grief for after,' Anna says, 'if there is some, but now I need to say an epitaph.'

We all look up to the sky. She says, 'He kept order, and his prices – they were always right. Wild parties too – and look!' she turns to us, 'Honour, respect as well. They've taken off his bellyband.' And so they have. 'I'll take those flintlocks, though,' she says, and doing so she slips her prize book in his shirt. He's golden bristly like a boar.

'You'll take some of those hairs,' says Maas. 'They are a talisman.'

'Where'll we put him?' Omar asks. 'The river, that's the place.'

I think – *I run to the rock ... I run to the river.*
Hmmm – maybe there's an opera there. Smugglers,
bandits and liberators – they keep cropping up like
golden barley, betrayals, arias – maybe I could try my
luck ...

'No, no, don't take him down,' says Vlad. 'He'll
be all over us.' He's pinned with knives they throw in
circuses – two that have done for him, others stuck in
the tree, like petals round.

'No, no, don't bother me,' shouts Daria, when she
hears – 'I'm busy moving chairs. Don't put him in the
river, or they'll know it's you, Omar. Besides, one
person to a grave – that is the rule.'

'I didn't know you loved me so,' Anna says to me.
'To settle Zef.'

'Those circus knives,' I say, 'they seem to give a
clue.'

'That's rather obvious, you know,' she says.

'I only pulled a string,' I say.

'You made a judgement,' Maas shouts out, 'and
you pulled two strings. The red, the green. Your dead
hand – it maybe didn't throw the knives – but all the
rest ...'

'Oh yes, the rest,' shouts Vlad. 'That makes us suffer – terror is the rest, it's sending guys to jail and death for what they cannot know and cannot change. The rest is bits that you can't fuse. Look at me, how I come from a place, call it a country, that's only made of parts. Capitalism, now – that is wall to wall, it's true equality, it lets us all see each as he, she, is. The struggle then belongs to all.'

'Well,' says Anna, 'capitalism's not what we have here. We are a zone of transit. Now my dead love is journeying – North, South – who knows where he'll end up? We should have buried him, not left him on that tree. He'll haunt us ... Maybe not an admirable guy. A leader, though ...' and Vlad has put his arms around her,

'Anna, come to me, and be with me. We can't be equal, but we could pretend to be. Nothing is equal, nor equivalent. You make a proposition – and it falls at once. Too many motives, perhaps none's effective. Will each tree have its bandit pinned and judged?'

'I doubt it, Vlad,' says Maas. 'I'm from a tiny country, no one thinks he, she, is equal to the others.'

'Maas,' says Vlad. 'You're superficial. When one finds a thought that seems to be impenetrable – you must push through. There always is another side – you take your pilgrim's stave, you beat the leaves, the branches, down. It takes a hundred years – but then, you see another landscape ...'

'Vlad,' asks Anna, 'do you really love me? It seems strange, there was no sign, and no desire. You were an artist – now you're just a mystery.'

'Quiet, idiots!' says Omar. 'Love, punishment – you think you hold the key, and yet the clues don't fit the motives. I'm the one who knows – vendetta, rivalry. That's the force. That guy Zef, his own people did for him, and now they'll come for us.'

'If we did it,' Maas says, 'it would have been for justice. Bad guy. But – because he upset order? Or is his death itself disorderly, disordering? What happens now? When justice is done, what has it accomplished? Does everything all start again, unchanging, undiminished?'

'Why not?' asks Vlad. 'When we are sure what justice is – go to! Give it to everyone! No discount, no exceptions.'

'If the pinning up was done by you,' Maas points at me, 'it seems a crime of passion – or else, of altruism. Saving Anna – was that so unselfish? She didn't want salvation. Or was it just rules of a game – quite arbitrary, doing what we told you? Not thinking of the consequence?'

'Come on,' shouts Daria. 'Forget that stuff. It's showtime, five minutes, and you're on.'

'Your time has come, you lads,' says Omar.
'Hand out the prizes, and the strings – see what they're
joined to, treats or tricks.'

They do the show. There's lots of circus. Like old
monarchies – on the high-wire, there's the kings.
Generals fired from their howitzers. We the jester
clowns, with tigers round.

It's classy stuff they do, Vlad, Maas. A break with
wry modernity. No more the concepts, no more irony
and worn-out girders tied with raffia – it's heavy now.
Up on the stage, like in a pantomime, goes the stooge:
– you do analysis – no, not of you yourself, but of Karl
Marx, of Kant, of Jean-Jacques. Other monsters too.
Hobnobbing with them, pulling coloured strings that
may reward or kill – over and over.

'Maybe I'm the prize,' says Anna 'But Vlad
shan't have me, though.'

I say, 'Be very careful, all of us! Zef had interests,
I am sure. A minister? A brigand?'

'Mainly, he sold cars,' says Daria. 'They drove on
territory, though, that belongs to him.'

The riggers do their flim-flam. Omar says,
'These guys don't travel round, you know.
They're invited.'

'What's the strangeness in all that?' asks Anna.
'There's politeness come into the world, Omar. You
kill, you judge – by invitation only.'

'Let's not exaggerate,' says Omar. 'They're artists, they discriminate. It isn't massacres or empires – it's just fun, up on the stage. Or up a tree.'

I say, 'They might sort out another little problem, Omar. Jim, washed clean, in his own blood – might rise again and give us all a stir. Maas and Vlad, they're quick with ropes – and given all the elephants they'll have followed, with spades and buckets too.'

'No,' he says, and pulls his silver lock. 'They're artists, and unpredictable, though they'll want their fees.'

'Zef!' says Anna. 'He was my man, so I should have a say. Not just a lover I have lost – an income too. They say justice was done – should I feel glad or sad?'

Omar says, 'I haven't had my justice yet. I'm not too bothered, either.' He puts his arm round Anna, and slides the clothes from round her shoulders, 'Poor half sister. Here there's lots of halves that's looking for their wholes,' he says.

'Back to your forest hideout,' Anna says, and smacks him on the nose.

They bicker on. There's a concert down the road, part of the festival. Daria floats between the shows. The concert's opera – they're in plimsolls, they read their parts. There's a wind machine. I think – that looks an easy thing, I could do that ... And so transform my life, relation to the world. Another guy is doing it. There's a thunder sheet as well.

'Be a love,' shout Daria towards me – 'Stack up those empty chairs, they spoil the scene.'

We stand outside, and listen. 'Zef could watch the love – they always have it in the operas,' Anna says to me, 'Maybe that's why you come.'

'Zef made his deals here, in the intervals,' I say. 'It was a classy scene.'

'We should go back, says Anna. 'Though Maas and Vlad are such a tacky pair. The music is so large, and we're so small.'

'Anna,' I say. 'You're lost. The music has no size. And we are rooted here ...'

'Not lost,' she says, 'I'm hunting.' Then she shouts and pulls – 'Don't get in that car,' and there's some tricksters, beckoning me in, and pulling too.

'Just a hundred metres up the rise,' one shouts.

'They're my friends,' Anna says, 'but you mustn't answer questions from them. Why not let's go into the music?'

I say, 'It's old stuff, Anna, all dressed down.'

'Zef never went unless it was full costume. Period. And patchouli. He was like you,' she says.

Then another car – covered in ads and numbers – passes us. It's cops. Inside there's Daria, she says, 'It's Jim. They found his clothes. No body ...' and away she goes: she cries, 'Just save the shows ...' and she is gone.

She looked so beautiful, captive there – young again, as young as me. Must be the fear that makes us so.

There's Omar, throwing rocks at cars, leaping up and down, and shouting ...' Doing his mad act,' Anna says, and turns away.

Then, running down the road – here's Maas and Vlad. It seems they're being chased – there's crowds behind, some guys in suits, all angry as red ants ... Too many questions, people tired of answering. Someone got fingered – or they thought they were.

'It's not sex, it's politics,' says Anna, though I didn't doubt it.

The crowds mingle, the angry, the relieved, the gangsters and the music lovers. The opera has paused, it seems, and here's the people, some leaving briskly, and for good, others waiting for another round.

I say, 'An act has ended.'

Some time later, Daria returns. She says to me, 'Jim's clothes left them cold. I had to tell them you'd been doing bad deals with Zef. That will give you some respect.'

She makes me cover for Zef's dubious deals.

I am a boss, with henchmen, if I need. I run the arts, and run the traffic too. I have foot soldiers, though I'll never tell.

Omar says to me, 'Watch what you say. Your tall stalk attracts the scythe.'

'I don't want the kind of light you've put me in,' I tell Daria. 'Stick to your own truths.'

Vlad and Maas are still around: they haven't had their pay. They don't go in for truth – it's rather the procedures.

These shows – there's no more continuity. Daria takes them from a catalogue – operas, symposia, a Swanee whistle group, tattoos and massages ... if ever there was sense, it's blasted thoroughly to scraps. It's good. I can't stand things just the same or similar. The tourists come and go – a show an evening, sometimes dances with those swords.

'If you take over, organise, and pocket cash,' says Daria to me. 'We're stuck with Vlad and Maas. It's theirs, the money. But they can pass the nights somewhere, and dole out justice in the street. And you will do Zef's deals.'

This sounds like paradise, though Omar spoils the view. It's paradise, not Eden, so perhaps the snakes are in a different garden, though there's no one left to ask.

Being boss is easy: you say yes or no. Don't make a count – either way there's some keen guy will do your will. 'What if I guess it wrong?' I ask, and Daria says scornfully,

'Whatever happens, it will not last long. Remember, if your end should hurt, you'll have no memory of it, no memory at all. And if you end up on a tree like Zef – it's all a show. You're quite indifferent, it's like acting in some literature, the effect is on the rest, not you. You just hang there, and guys will come, take back the uniform, the knives – and you won't feel a thing.'

In fact, they take Zef's body, leave the props, the tribute, the romance.

I bring in operas of many kinds – there's landing on the moon, and falling in the sun, and star-crossed this and starstruck that. Some choruses are slung on hooks and upside down they sing. There's profuse sex, the plays spill off the stage and sit on laps, poke pins in ears. There is applause, but not from all. Everything's a success, at once, or some time other. The shows move on, they leave a tiny rind in memories, like moons left out to wither in the sun.

Maas and Vlad – they stay. They are in residence. No one outside invites them, so they don't leave. Heavy conceptual stuff – it's over, and the prancing too, condescension to an audience, as if the shards all matter, even to fortune.

I'm working on a piece – an orchestra of bush pianos – those should come in, and lots more. Africans to play them, then disappear.

A guy called Kili – one of my operatives, I guess. Never seen him before. A centurion, they're called. He says,

'No, no – not miniature stuff. You should get into something major. You're an anarchist, I can see. Some places, you go to jail just for thinking it. It lasts a second, the idea. Pure. And anarchy, once thought, it fades and moves away. The echo stays with you for ever, though,' quite shocked, he ends, 'It means that you deny the sacred.'

The idea for my great piece, it circles, lands screaming like a seagull, in my head: 'Yes, Kili, you're right,' I say. 'The thought is in me. It must be great, be grandiose. It's called, 'Footprints in the Sea'. And suddenly, it's gone! Now, what's the deal?'

He starts to tell. It's like one of Omar's fantasies, of hiding, jumping out. More money bought with frightening.

'No, no,' I say, 'I am the boss, of bad things I just draw the outline. What you mad dogs do – I don't want to hear, still less to know. It's up to you, to square your animality with what you shouldn't do.'

Daria's right. When you do festivals, the pretty women hug you, and some kiss. The agents slip you tips. Now, we've a landscape, made of wire, plasters left over. You could make it a country. Then I laugh – we've a country already. Anna still lives alone. I guess I'm now her man, protector, part of my job. On her wall, there's a long picture of her, nude. It's hard not to look at that.

She says, 'That's what it's for, so people won't stare at me.' I say,

'It works like that. It's the same with me – I'm not really boss. There's just a picture that you look at ...' and she interrupts,

'Of course that's what you are, a boss. There's bosses everywhere, and when one goes, another one pops up, like targets in a booth. It's not a quality. Just a position.'

Daria says loudly to me, 'Solve the problem! Pictures on walls.'

Someone has painted on a church wall – God, chasing Adam from the garden, waving a castrating knife. A jealous God indeed – if you design an Eve, you'd want her for yourself.

'So what, Daria?' I ask, 'It seems quite ludic. These tales – drawn out into fine threads, so many times. It's true my guys are straight in religious things. It's wisest not to paint on walls. Best keep it in the head, even the fantasies.'

Daria says, 'It's publicity, for sure. We don't want stuff about us, though, not the anthropology. Just the art, and leave the traffic out.'

'Omar says there's money in it. And fame. I don't know who it's for,' I say.

'He's just a dirty devil,' Daria says. 'I'd sooner he was taking parties up, into the woods, than pondering in my bed.'

'If he wasn't my brother, half of him, I'd take him on myself,' says Anna, playing safe.

I think how every string quartet must have its dirty devil, the viola sometimes it will be, who leads you up, away, into the woods, the pines wet and thronging round, fingers on your neck. 'Hush, there!' says Daria, sharply, to me, 'You don't know the first thing. You're a front man, I made you boss. Don't look behind the flats.'

The churches here are open to the air, just like they say the Turks had left them, or by mere neglect; the friezes sprouting toadstools, the saints' haloes golden turbans, faces white, the heads decapitate, the features all the same.

There's a raised tomb – a girl, she looks quite mad, they're passing her over, under. Maybe she'll get cured.

'They tried that on me too,' says Anna: 'I was scared, not cured.'

'It all seems inconclusive, these beliefs the guys have here,' I say. 'Though if you haven't gold, you may as well fight over history.'

'This painting over – doesn't happen much,' says Anna. 'It must impact, but you will never see the ones who say they care, believe. It's Omar's world – most things are open secrets, and you mustn't pry. Or tell.'

'My guys come from all angles – they all converge,' I say. 'The traffic – cash, some suffering – serves to stop their suffering. Some talisman to keep you safe, cure your sick head. Appease the legions that stand grey behind each act.'

'Of course I love you,' Daria says to me. 'I know what you know. You're always round. The sad thing is – you've no responsibility – but you will take a load of consequence.'

'Like Jim,' I think I say.

'It's all a context,' Daria says. 'No one's really in command. Not for long, that is.'

'Of course I love you,' Anna says. 'You're always where I'd find you, but you're not around. You don't impinge. It's you, you're well chalked-in, defined. That's you – pulled up to the stage when shows are done.'

There's love around, it seems: it doesn't help at all. I'm still responsible for what I haven't done, and what the others do. Anna's dismissive, and she says,

'Don't think about responsibility, all that mystic stuff. It's what you are that sets you up, and that's your part, and if they look for you, they rarely get it wrong. You could go somewhere else, and join another tale,

but if you don't – the story's here, you have to follow
it.'

I say, 'It wasn't great before, it's not great now, I
know. Wait – this guy,' I show the catalogue, 'he
wants a hectare to lay out his stuff. We could have
planted something there. This one – eviscerates a
piano, sticks all kinds of things inside, where there
were strings. Things sounding, some alive, most dead.
I fear this phase is coming to an end. The fogeys will
come back, there'll be an ice age of frames and
pedestals ...'

She is not interested: she says,

'It was terrible before. Like I said, now, it's just
after.'

I say to comfort her – radiant, disgruntled as she
is,

'The chiefs – they never know. If they thought,
they could suspect,' and Vlad creeps up, and with a
flourish says,

'We only look at consequences, you know.
Intentions, blindness – really, those don't count.'

'Oh no!' says Daria. 'Consequences have nine
lives. You'll be here for ever, you and Maas. Now, I
want you gone, paid what you think you're owed, or
not.'

'We know how to end an act,' says Vlad,
annoyed. 'You guys are quite exposed. Act two will

end with deaths and flight, exchange of names, paternities.'

'Look at the trees!' cries Maas. 'The world will come and peer. The dodgy deals will be revealed!'

He's right. Omar has cut the trees. We were so used to the forest, the wet pines, we hadn't seen a thing – now it's a photo, grey on grey. Set up, and huge – bigger and prettier than before – more ominous, less wet. Behind, the trunks are bound with chains, trucked off. Shelters too, and bones.

'Those gloomy trees!' shouts Daria. 'Each one a stake in someone's flesh. Away, away ... the cleansing, purity!'

Walking up and down – I recognise Kili. He says, 'It's the spilling over. From life to other lives. It's not liked. Once, you could hide behind those trees. Now, it's a photograph. The guys who went to church – they had their laugh when it was done, not during.'

I say, 'The spilling over isn't new.'

He shows me a piece in a collector's mag. There I am, in Zef's shirt, 'purveyor of human misery', it says.

That's the aesthetics! Then there's the love story – it seems me, with Anna. Daria strutting somewhere out of range. Trying to split us, with religion. Maas – or Vlad – must have written this, as their names don't appear. Omar's there too, like Loki, changing landscapes. Anna says,

'These stories in a story – all too twee. We all must keep our distances, otherwise we'll all leach into one another,' and I say,

'I'm just a blank in this, wearing others' clothes.'

'That is the best,' says Kili. 'Changing your shape is how it all begins.'

'Remember, Kili,' I tell him. 'I don't plot. I take advantage, that is all.' He salutes, and leaves.

Anna's thoughtful, then she says, 'I could go with Omar, now he's made clean sweep, his life all tidied up. No trees.'

'Don't let the incest bother you,' I say. 'Paternity's a slippery thing,' and she is quiet, and then,

'It's not attraction. It's the symmetry.'

I say, 'That's the best, too. It seems to mean a lot – the two by two.'

Omar takes me behind the photograph. The mound is grey and greasy.

'It has to be greasy,' Omar says, 'or we couldn't slide down it. See how much better it is, now, without the trees. And now I hear we're going to be related?' He turns his tumbled row of teeth towards me. Is Anna entering that graveyard? I wonder.

Omar takes my hand – 'Up we go!' he says. 'You've trouble with your people. Some want to be my people.'

'Why do you ask?' I say. 'Kili keeps bothering me. But – you know, I've no people. I keep my distance.'

'I didn't ask a question,' Omar says. 'It is so. You've trouble now, although you see it only in the future.'

We climb up – there's little rectangles, black in the grey, the sleeping huts, and rounds for making charcoal. The pits where there were roots are shallow, shell holes. It's steeper now, we slide and fall, we turn grey and darker grey. 'Come on,' he shouts, 'higher, higher, or you won't get down so fast.'

At the top – there is no top. I make the gesture to the sun, but it is not around, beyond this top there's other tops, and more into the mist. Grey trees.

'You sit on this,' he says, as if I couldn't guess. It's black plastic, for the bin. He sits behind, and down the slippery slope we go – 'Shout!' he shouts, 'you have to shout and scream, or it's no fun!'

We shriek as if we're hunters flushing game, and down we go, we only think of grey, grey up, below; descent is like a birth of worlds, the new, the terrible ones, unexplored, already full of airy creatures. It's rough space, chewing your bones.

'Omar,' I shout, 'what, when we can't go beyond?'

We can't take off, there's nowhere we can fly – the market, trucks, people walking as they do. We know it all.

'You'll see,' he says – and then we hit, except there is no impact, we are through the photograph, we've stopped, we are not safe. It's not conclusive, not at all.

'There!' he says. 'Now you are cleaner, even more pure. If not, there's something wrong with you.'

So, of course, I can't say I feel the same, and being grey with mud besides. 'Yes, Omar, it's a novelty, this ride. You'd make it an attraction for your country,' and he says, 'It's yours as well, this country, since we shall be relatives. If I'm with Anna, that means you are related too, and to the country also, that's by law.'

The precision dancers are here. One seems to forget his moves. The music sounds like vomiting. They all wear baseball caps, and strut – all that practice, military moves. They've got the whole town rocking, on big screens, miming them, their left – the others' right.

'I shan't ask them back,' I say.

'You don't ask anyone back,' says Daria. 'They're clean. Tidiness, is what I ask. The dirt pushed out of sight.'

'They ought to depilate,' I say. 'That hair is out of place.'

They put up a slide – Hiroshima, I think. It seems quite out of place.

'Everybody's dancing,' Daria says. 'Business is good. Why don't you start another branch somewhere? Paris?'

'No, Daria, I must keep my eyes on something here. The tidiness is all,' I say. 'I'll need to push the dirt somewhere.'

Their lead guy grabs my arm and twirls me round. 'Fuck off,' I think, but shuffle round a bit. I say, 'Go light on the religious stuff, it's quite divisive still, though you'd not think ...'

'Hey,' he says, 'we're a clean act. No offence.'

Who cares?

'Kili,' I say, 'I thought – something for the guys. You know – those horses, bronze, in Venice. I could set some up for us. They're copies – there are only copies left.'

'Yes,' he says, 'I'm sure they'd like something, and appreciate. Not horses, though, they're too much work.'

'Of course,' I say, 'I should have thought.' We need to be together, close. When you're together, you can keep a secret longer.

'We must settle things with Omar,' I tell Kili. He says,

'You might talk to him.'

'You know,' I say, 'I speak a southern dialect. I'm not always well understood.'

'It must be settled,' Kili says.

'Naturally,' I say. 'We're not a parliament, we don't take votes. What's to be done – it's done.'

He persists. 'We must bring him back. There's too much fooling. Plots, not just a taking of advantage.'

'I suppose so,' I say, drawing it out, the talk; it isn't necessary: 'He should see a dentist. Fix that smile.'

'"Human misery"?' I say to Maas: 'That's what you say I bring? They mean the shows? Often it's true – but then, those dancers, Japanese, I guess, they'll come. It should be fun. And justice, Maas? We're under occupation still. You can't take risks, and make a judgement, get it wrong and find there's no way back.'

Omar is settled. He's used to being captain, having a band. Now, there's quiet around him.

Then Daria says, 'I must be mayor. You must keep moving up, or else you're mulch.'

Into my adagio comes her percussion. Shouting, too.

'I'd rather be at that big station, with a choice of trains,' I say.

'No, no,' she says, 'you must enjoy it while it lasts, or else you're even sadder when it ends.'

'This is not the struggle,' I say. 'The one we talked of long ago. The Africans.'

'That's gone, you know it has,' she says. 'We must keep the people moving on, and moving through, the trucks as well, people making money as they can, us running what we can, and holding on.'

Crime and punishment, Maas and Vlad. 'If you pay us, we will leave,' they say.

'Stay around,' I say. 'You'll be of use if other acts don't show.'

Anna says to me, 'You're quite perverse. You're jealous now, you didn't want me when you could.'

'They'll not find gold on Omar's hill. We must keep people trucking through, and skimming off. Loyalty, at whatever cost. Things will go on getting difficult,' I say.

'They'll find a cure for it,' says Anna. 'Like they did for jealousy – it's everybody screwing everybody else.'

Sometimes I go and kneel in a small mosque nearby. It's like string quartets, without the noise.

Daria has said, 'When I get tall enough, I may have to stamp on you.'

'Remember Jim,' I say. 'I remember, if you don't, and your part in him.'

'Jim's clean,' she says. 'The river's acid, even the bones have gone down to the sea. It's all settled, Omar and Anna – a nice brick house, up on the ridge, where they can see everything.'

Tonight, there's a solo act – this dancer. Or maybe she just moves the lights, or sings. She's limbering, bending like a hinge, her act, I guess. 'I could stay here,' she says, 'selling the tickets, then moving up.'

'No, no,' I say, 'you are an artist. That's your slot. We employ only war victims, our menials, out to climb their hill again. They show you to your place.'

'My!' she says, 'what a glum view you have. I bet my story doesn't interest you? That has ugly things in, too.'

'No, no interest at all,' I say. I think her name is Mara. Face like a sleepy cat's. I'm in expansive mode, I say,

'I am the patron here. I bring you in, the tourists follow. Then, there are the prostitutes – they're quite fixed. Then, the tourists often look for maids and gardeners – those they find. To keep things smooth and orderly, you need an agency – which isn't arbitrary, like what Maas and Vlad put on, but some guy that knows the dialects. The guys obey ... I am the agent.'

'It all needs love,' says Mara.

'You don't look innocent,' I say.

'No, you don't listen. I said love, not innocence,' she says.

Her act's not bad. She's chosen music to go with the movement – something about Carmelites, revolution, and beheadings. It lets you think of something else.

If she falls, it doesn't show. Maybe it's a part of it, the act. She flings herself around, quite rhythmically. It makes you feel – joyful, free.

Perhaps we could bend my rule, and hire her. Smarter than Anna, always looking for the better life, painting the past one black and grey.

Without the trees, there is more light.

Here's a new guy, Kavad. 'Where's Kili gone?' I ask.

'He didn't know the side he's on. He had to be let go. You had some troubles – there were foreigners, and practices you said you didn't understand. Betting on sport – childish, you said.'

'Yes, yes,' I say. 'That's it, quite well expressed. You know – our money's cheap. It goes to someone's debt, so we don't seem to keep cash for ourselves. They say we have the best part. Letting people who have nothing make their way, from places where there's nothing you can eat or dig.'

'It's true,' says Kavad. 'We should be thankful, each for each. We're low risk, real profits, too. It's old style, but we'll beat the new arrivals.'

Old style ...

Mara says, 'The paintings of the paradise, and then, those knives and their precision – makes you think. Some law and order – getting sums just right.'

I say, 'We manage here quite well. But you – you look so eagerly at every scene, you want to join it on to all the rest, and make a story. It is not like that.'

'I know,' she says. 'You have to break the sequences. That's why I'm running. But you're wrong about my act – it doesn't hook to anything.'

'Most who come here are like that,' I say. 'That is their worth. We all do what we must, and if there's knives – it's for the cash, honour, loyalty, the things that make tomorrow's sense.'

'I watch the storks,' says Mara. 'That's where my dance comes from. Hares – they have their art as well. It's to do with food and sex, ephemeral I guess; not progress.'

'Since you mention it,' I say, 'of course, there's dreadful things I must contribute to, it's all to keep things moving through. We are a transit zone, of course, and we don't know where people come from, where they go. But dreadful things – they usually happen far away. And certainly – the bad is always unintentional. That doesn't make it good, of course; it takes it somewhere we're all used to dealing with. Not far, not near, not good or bad, but moving on, and doing what we must.'

I think – oh no, don't let there be a summoning of Maas and Vlad! They put the strings right in your hand, and you must choose which one to pull – and life or death it is. Quite arbitrary. For Mara too.

'The food here – it's like home, a little,' Mara says. 'There's some people remembers even a few words of the language I used to speak.' She twirls and pouts: 'I'm too heavy to lift now. I'm normal.'

'So,' I say, 'you are in transit. You see, I keep the borders here. It's like a park with animals. I stop my beasts from eating those who come by boat, and of course, they mustn't eat each other. Then there's the ones who're transiting ...'

We watch a group that's been trucked in and traded, ready to be trucked off somewhere else. They don't look pleased.

'Mara,' I say, 'see, they're all alive. It's true life here's not so smooth – but everywhere is full of people living with some guys that they don't like, who maybe beat them too, and guys who go down mines or in the sea, and bring up jewels and don't get paid. I have to keep my people loyal – it's like an army, like the soldiers were back then, before the states, and motivation.'

'I understand all that,' says Mara, though it seems she'd like to make a discourse of it, everything that is.

Up on the ridge, the brick house, Omar's and Anna's, seems to shift, the lines are shimmering, their tin chimney drops.

'Oh no,' shouts Mara, and there's lots who watch – it slides, and recomposes as it speeds, no longer habitable, of course, but pink and orange, strings of brick and rubble, flattening out, determined – then it rests where we can't see, behind the photograph.

'I'm quite in awe,' says Daria, who's run up and gawps. 'Those colours! Maybe Omar wasn't in, that would be luck.' She says, 'Of course, you build brick houses and you think there's no bad wolves can blow them down – but now, those little piggies, Anna, her brother too – they'll learn they mustn't trust their grannies' tales.'

'There!' I say to Mara. 'Now, there is calm. It's happened – not to you. There's luck. Dear Anna – maybe if I'd known her more, I'd have been sleeping in that house....It's a relief – the slide has happened, nothing has gone for ever – even the bricks can be re-used. People get their punishment, it all speeds on the plot, the lovers take a pace that brings them close together, closing to the happy end.'

'I don't see any lovers here,' says Mara. 'Not that it bothers me.'

She pokes at the pile of bricks. 'What a disaster,' she says. 'These poor people. Their dignity. Their experience, their suffering, the loss that surely cripples them.'

'You can do nothing. Nor can they,' I say. 'I'm the man who brings in hi-pop. It smooths things out. And there's the trade. You need the trade to purge, to move things on, and cover up. You must!'

She's not convinced.

I say, 'It takes, say, fifty years. Like Jim, looking for his proof. I'm sure that it will come. Fame, too.'

'Who's Jim?' she asks.

'He thought he could be boss,' I say, waving my hands: 'He'll come back, in fifty years. Up the river from the sea, a salmon.'

She stands and stares at the rubble of the house: 'You Russians,' I say. 'You don't run, as all the others would. You stand like oxen waiting for the bolt.'

'I'm a Russian who runs,' she says.

We pull Anna from the ruin: she looks back up the long slide of mud: 'What a pain,' she says, 'you see, it was a solid house. I've not a mark, just the memory to come.'

It's clear that Omar's not around. Anna says, 'Omar will be back, he'll wait till he thinks he's safe.'

'Who's Omar?' Mara asks.

'Someone who isn't here,' says Anna. I suppose she's still alarmed.

'Another act's arrived,' I say. 'You think it's ended, well or bad, then up they spring, and want applause.'

'More opera!' Daria cries. 'It has the lot!' Eyeing Mara up and down, she says, 'Too plump, my dear. It's that sour cream. I'm coming to prefer a trans – I hear your country has a train that's full of them. Now Omar's gone, the naughty boy, for me, sex is a metaphor; or else it's full as stuffed eggs.'

'No, Daria,' I say. 'Restraint – think of those Japanese storks – they do the dance, then settle down for sixty years. The Trans was just an idle joke ...' but she persists, she says to Mara,

'Siberia, now. I gather that too has everything – it's empty, except for cities and the wells ...'

'There is room for you,' says Mara, much taken with Daria. 'It's now a refuge, Siberia, there's the train, and riches everywhere.'

'Yes!' Daria says, pulling at Mara's arms. 'Yes, we could flee, and I'd escape responsibilities here, the mud, the grey, and these dull folks ...'

'No, Daria,' Mara says, and laughs. 'It's what I'm fleeing from.'

It's an impasse.

Daria, at a loss, shouts at me, 'Your trouble is, you fit words to everything – even those silly string quartets.'

I say, 'But Daria, opera is full of words, even if you can't hear them. Besides, you're mayor – a house has fallen down, what now?'

Daria insists, 'Operas come ready made, there's no invention there, straight up and down. Now – who built that house illegally upon a hill? My dear,' she turns to Anna, who's still white and silent, 'Can you pay a fine?'

Anna says, 'Daria, you have the preoccupations of an orthodox saint,' and Mara looks at the two of them with admiration: 'Things have been unsettled since Zef ...' Anna concludes, and turns back into her void.

'Of course they are,' says Daria. 'When one falls, the balance of the rest is disturbed – probably for ever. That is the basis of humanism, not that it settles anything. Zef was executed in the name of justice – though Maas applies it quite arbitrarily. We know he sighted on the right target – and Vlad might have missed with his knives. Everything is just, just right. That's my philosophy – it is pragmatic and idealistic at once, if you're concerned.'

I thought it was Daria did for Zef. Oh well, there's guilt, and there's retribution – and then, another horseman, skulls on his bridle – that's punishment. The sound of the hooves is stunning.

'Look, you guys, just keep talking. I have to set up the new act,' I say.

I must bear these people along, I must bear with them, till the moment when they must be dropped, that's life and not life.

Here's the bus, more hopeful guys, looking for things here to criticise and expose.

'There's lots of you,' I say. 'I don't know where to put you.'

'There's the other nine buses, trying to get up the road,' says the guy, Georg.

'Did you put these numbers in your leaflet?' I ask. 'And what's it called, your piece?'

'It's called "The Priests",' the guy says, surprised. 'No quotations, no fine writing, no memorable lines, no fiery characters. We wanted it staged here, because we heard the whole place now is run by criminals, and we wanted that to spill over to our text.'

'You expect too much,' I say. 'You need to put your implicit stuff into your stuff. Not much spills over, you need some guslar to make dead men into heroes.'

Georg doesn't take this in – he says,

''The music – we have engineers, they set it up. It's all prepared – seeds in pods, shaken, pearls dropped onto teak. Birds – lots of those, in various activities. We have a live guy, a musician. He plays the sitar – it's the only instrument devoid of spirit, that denotes only the movements of time – fast time, slow time. The rest is living things, passing their existences in nature. That way, you don't need scenery, or clocks. So, the performance can go on and on, until it's done. Deaths and discourses – they will take the time it takes.'

'I need to write some notes, on what it's all about,' I say. 'It can't be about everything.'

'There's this seminar, conference, full of priests,' Georg explains. 'They argue, they have different gods, and various faiths. The evidence for each – is slender. There are quarrels, polemics, the nights are full of fire, the days of soot. And in the end, the faith is lost by all. Since faith is personal, they lose themselves. They search for something else, beliefs collective, and infectious ...'

'Whoa that horse!' I shout. 'This religious stuff – here, it is dynamite. Back in your bus!'

'No, no,' he says. 'Not religion. It is history.'

'That too!' I say. 'Leave it alone. We've worked it out – the distribution of our power. You do your sums, and dole it out according to resource. Then, all you need, is maintaining the equilibrium, coming down tough on any who usurp ...'

'Let me go on,' says Georg. 'These faithless guys – they feel they must do good. There is this village girl – let's call her Inge: she's taken with the love these guys can offer her. and, well, she falls, like women used to once – the villagers divide into their sides – and this destroys the village. The "priests" – spoiled thoroughly, of course – they race, like white wolves, over her soft body. I know – we must be careful, very, very careful with all this. Anywhere but here – it goes down well. You see – the show is not about belief, it's about loss, and how destructive that will be.'

'Yes, yes,' I say, impatient. 'But the answer is, you need to get beliefs – and then they're lost, collectivity's destroyed – and so – belief, just like its loss, destroys. It's dog that follows dog.'

'Exactly so,' shouts Georg. He's delighted. 'Yes! You see the paradox. It all goes on and on, so does the show – we've made it stretch for days. It's hopeful and it's hopeless, at the same time. That's it! What endures – is time, that ticks away, the sitar...you can understand.'

'I'll find the sitar guy a chair,' I say. 'Your engineers can crawl about. It troubles me – your show, it's trite, generic. Loss. Circles. Can't the priest-things represent say – styles of leadership? Wrong ways to make your fortune?'

'Don't laugh before you've seen it,' says Georg. 'There's energy to spare – when they cast down their gods, and spirits rise up to the trees ... the noise! The screams, the burning ...'

'Maybe your sitar guy sits on the floor?' I say. This show – it will not do at all, and still full buses grind on up the hill.

The crews spill out, the villagers and virgins too. 'Now, have no fear,' says Georg. 'We have our fun. We scream, we shout, we tear at eyes and limbs, we rain down fire and call up floods ...'

'No booze, no throwing food,' I say.

'I thought we'd play before the *bons bourgeois*, who know it all, what to expect, the discourse and the noise?' says Georg.

'That's true,' I say. 'But to ensure you've a full house, we let the locals in for free – they take it rather seriously ...'

The show's magnificent. It's circuses and tragedy, there's marching bands and pompom girls, there's massed trombones and string quartets, it lasts three days – and then goes on ... there's a Mercutio, his

99

death repeated in his deathless mode, there's dromedaries, dancers who are Japanese storks that promise yin and yang, all done with taste and text, with glancing referents, with collages, with nod and wink at quotes, and themes that come and go ... There's slides of houses falling down and blowing up, of massacres and famines, purges, meditation. There is no booze, no drugs, no throwing food. The players rampage through the town, our work is stopped – there's everything, and nothing too. The public comes and goes, and some crawl on the stage and sleep.

Daria says, 'Well, Jim was right, we wasted time with politics. We should have put our tap-shoes on and had some fun.' I say,

'Now, Daria, that comes close to sarcasm. There is no room for philistines. Times change, and we must watch as they slide by.'

Omar goes screaming through the town. Something must be done.

I say to Daria, 'This show – it could be Jim's proof.'

Maas says, 'What Jim got, was hardly justice.'

'Without justice, you can't say what he got was punishment,' says Vlad.

'I don't see it matters,' Mara says.

'Of course it does,' says Anna. 'People go on about it all the time. That's what you're supposed to calculate with, the right, the wrong, the doing and its consequence.'

'Jim was a pain,' says Daria. 'I've said so many times. But if he'd just got lost ... Even making noise, like Omar. Instead, he asked for it. Not his proof, but genuine surprise. Trusting some crazy guy who had a pointed steel!'

'That's quite reactionary, you know,' says Mara. 'Surprise is often good. And trust is sacred, so they say.'

'Well,' says Anna briskly, 'Jim's gone. Maybe the proof went with him. Why don't we get these actors here, to do the show over and again – replace the sword dance too? It's more cosmopolitan. It should last. There's girls and boys, entwined. And tap – like I should like to learn.'

'That's right, that's true, Anna,' Daria says. 'There's something in tap that makes you think of incest. It's how they look down at their feet when they don't need to.'

'Don't provoke me,' Anna says.

Daria is furious, she laughs, 'Why, I could pull your head off like an owl's!'

Anna runs screaming through the town.

'Daria! You don't say that to Anna, nuisance though she is!' says Mara.

'Anna and Omar – they're a pair,' says Daria.

'We know,' says Mara, 'But we should know something more than that – about the conflict, and the things that Maas and Vlad deal in. See if it matters after all.'

'You'll not find that from me,' says Daria, mock-kindly, 'nor from him.' She points at me. 'We keep things turning, that is all.'

'Everybody's looking for something,' Mara chants, 'that's what the song says.'

'I didn't recognise it,' I say.

'It's not my real job, singing,' Mara says, 'I did some journalism.'

'Everybody has,' I say.

'Well,' she says, 'I'll stick around you, as you are a boss. But I've in mind to go much further. So don't expect my intimacy. I'd like to know – how do you eliminate your guys? And the trade – doesn't it make for suffering?'

'Of course, if I hurt people personally, I'd not be boss,' I say. 'You see, it is the general interest, call it a desire, that trade goes on. Like every other place, there's those exploited, treated bad. That's not the aim, it is a consequence, of interests, and doing what the others do, until we all live happily.'

'Your guy Kavad,' says Mara. 'You should watch him. People round him disappear – and then pop up again without their features. He cracks them, like lobsters.'

'It's the music,' I say. 'He comes to shows and listens to the noisy bits. It's hard to call it a philosophy. He wriggles in his seat as if he's peppers in his bum. Then he goes off .... It's not necessary, unless you're fragile. Or, I guess, inspired. The shows I bring – they're full of deaths. You'd think they'd be enough, but no, they prick the appetite. There's nothing I can do. The culture's predicated upon that. Settle your scores, or love your enemy. Try that – the loving ... Maybe painting's easier to fit into a frame, and keep it there, and sort its lineage.'

'It doesn't seem to bother you,' says Mara, wheedling.

'No, it doesn't much,' I say. 'I've other things ...'

'You're a saint,' says Daria to me, 'trying to do least evil. Or just seeing it. This place has always been a slave route, Mara, even when we all came out of Africa. Other days and other times ... You could do a little exhib about it. People love stories, always have – that's what we're famous for.'

Mara seems troubled, so I say, 'It's true, we do a little contraband. Everybody does, or has. States do it, or they don't. Here, I'm the state.'

'There's Daria too,' says Mara. 'Hurting and deaths.' I say,

'Daria's run out of people, Mara, she can only count on votes. We're divided on the big idea, Daria and I. On whether there is one, whether it's the same for all, and for the two of us.'

Georg comes up to us. He says, 'We want asylum, and passports. And to stay for ever, doing our show.'

I say, 'You can have asylum, or passports. Not both. Besides, I hate your show. It's like reason and mathematics – they all make cells with bars and locks.'

He's downcast: 'That's because our show's like yours, what's set up here. That's why you hate it.'

'I'm transitional,' I say. 'It's you who are the fascists. Stuck here.'

'You can do better than this,' Mara says to me, squinting up, and looking appetising, or trying to. I say,

'That's extravagant, what you say. Stupid, too. This is the best, for me. I'm perfectly balanced, and I'm the top. Every tree, every cock, needs its crest, and that's me.'

'Yes,' says Mara, 'but think of Kili. He didn't finish well – the ending took so long, he'll remember it for ever.'

'It's true,' I say, expansively. 'I was interested in justice. How mostly, we don't deserve it, and then Vlad and Maas showed there's no one good enough to dole it out.'

'It wasn't justice, I remember it,' says Daria, overhearing. 'It was the good; at least, that was on the cover of the book.'

'He must have qualifications to deal with that,' says Mara, quite impressed.

'You guys – you think the thing is winding down – and then there's climax. Really, it's dwindling, time to go – we always call it climax,' I say.

'You must see,' Mara says to me. 'You haven't long to go. You're soft, and worse, you think the trade's beneath you.'

I say, 'You can't end something with a fugue. You have the fugue, and then you find a way to finish off – a theme, a dying fall ...'

'You'll get the dying fall,' says Mara, 'if you don't do the fugue.'

It's clear, it's all a plot, another one. Daria's solo, once again.

More people, in from the sea, into the light, our light. Shipped off, and lucky to be gone.

'It has to end with a bang, a fictional one,' says Mara. 'A big finale. All the smugglers, your clan – and Anna, Omar, both delivered.'

'What clan?' I ask. 'Everyone looks the same to me. There's much more light, quite dazzling, now the trees have gone. It's hard to pick out individuals.'

'Your friends can't stand your friends, that's all there is,' says Daria. 'All your soldiers gathering, a triumph. And look! here's Anna and Omar.'

They're slid in, bound, and squawking mad, or so they seem. It is an awkward, but a possible conclusion; quite wry, the lovers sing it to an close, but—

'I see no lovers here,' says Mara.

There's some of my soldiers, thin buttocks in their generous jeans. Braver than wolves.

'Go on!' Daria shouts at me. 'Show some authority, and sing!'

Kavad's promoted. His own choice. He steps forward: 'Now is your chance – away! and do whatever you have always wanted. Take her too,' he points at Mara. 'It's true, that when you leave, you're hunted scum, but here's the dawn, above the mount – take profit from it ...' and he promises the things that I don't want, like Mara, a new name ...

They rehearse Georg's show. We're all there to watch:

We all stand round, or lounge, or lie: – here come the mad twins, the grannie with her sash and chain, the bearers of the dance, of justice and of retribution. The dead are there of course, and choruses of villains, shapeshifters ... The sitar's rather thin for such a crowd, but Kavad shouts above the rustle and the chat – 'We have our big idea! The state – or we should say the states, as various as the pebbles on a beach – they do what we do – the trade, expulsions and assimilations. Much more too – occupying other states, defining faiths and enemies, declaring war and peace, voting and prisons, writing their histories, anthems and fireworks ... Well, we shall make the leap. We'll be a state.'

'The idea's terrible,' I say, 'but I could be the boss of that as well as what I am today.'

'No!' Kavad says. 'We see you as old style – nostalgia for the avant garde, this thing about the forest animals and carving wood. You are King Log – we are King Stork!'

'It's nonsense,' I say. 'Just go on paying the politicos – if you're one of them, it'll all end bad, you'll be in jail.'

'No, no,' he says. 'Our plan is bigger.'

'Not religion?' I ask. 'Historically, I guess, you could. To me, it's an illusion ...'

'No, no,' says Kavad. 'Not that at all.'

'I thought that I could stand it – the discipline, obeying. But not for long,' I say.

'No, no, a proper state,' he says. 'Not Vlad and Maas, and strings you pull, those stories too ...'

'Well,' I say, not much moved or interested: 'I'd better leave. I have an urge to see Siberia.' That way, I'll make my fortune on my own, Mara for sure won't come.

'Hold on,' says Kavad. 'You can't just slide off. You're the patsy, not us. You have to leave a token.'

Oh no, I think – the judgement could belong to Maas and Vlad. Kavad asks,

'A hand – that would be gross. And seems religious, too. You may have stolen, but you gave us shows, which have no price, and maybe have no value either. So, any cash that's robbed – evaporates at once. It finishes in ears and eyes. It does not cure, but doesn't make you deaf and blind.'

'That, Kavad, is another bad idea. Punishments must be conventional – my misdemeanour was historical ...'

'And so shall be your punishment!' he shouts. 'An arm! A leg! All brigands lose a piece – an eye, maybe. It gives them power. You can't just take the train and go, a suitcase, packed with reputation, anonymity. We'd nail you up, like Zef – but that's old hat.'

What can I lose? What part's least painful, least discomforting?

Kavad says, 'You're lucky, you don't play the clarinet. One limb will serve you well. Those concertos for the left hand – you're luck is good, so practise them! We'll take a right arm, and part friends as before.'

Georg says his troupe will follow me, the priests can be The Doctors, trying to fix my arm back on, and Mara says her Carmelites had lost their heads, that's worse – my arm can be worked in somewhere to the dance. It seems that all are sure my loss is just. 'Remember Oedipus,' says Daria, 'lost his eyes.'

'The incest thing – that wasn't me,' I say, but there's agreement that I cannot leave without a tribute left behind.

'You'll have the best counselling,' Kavad says, 'from Vienna if you want. And for the deed – Mara suggests the guillotine. We'll let you wear a sky-blue coat – or you could break with custom – a power suit, maybe.'

They cut it off. It didn't exactly hurt. It didn't exactly exist – it is a nothing among the other nothings packed up in oneself. Losing an arm is a forfeit for things done, and doesn't guarantee against some future loss.

'You didn't have a fling with Mara,' Daria says, who's not too interested in talking about my arm, 'but now, you're in the "after" stage, as if you had her, and it's over. It's the mix of longing and disillusion that she has for you – not really hatred, or dislike, but nostalgia for something intimate that's gone ...'

'Yes,' I interrupt, 'just like my arm. At all events, I've paid for all the bad deeds I've been ignorant of, and some I remembered, then forgot.'

'We can't shake hands,' says Kavad, 'but welcome all the same. Look – here's some fun, I've found this picture in a symbol book. *Le bras armé!* See – it's your arm, and holds a mace. It's a pun – linguistic, visual, both at once. It can be our sign, in this we'll have our victory.'

'If you say so,' I say, primly. 'But you need more than that, to be a president, a boss. A master. You need to know about the spheres, their music too. There's talk of happiness, of markets, and of seeing you paid less.'

'We have a market here,' he says, 'and all the other stuff – well, if you say so. But that's is not my job. My task is doing things, not knowing them.'

'You've Daria to plot against,' I say.

'We'll throw that bitch some bones – clean ones, old ones,' and he laughs. 'I need to build high buildings, towers maybe. And string a wire, and Mara dances up there – maybe Vlad and Maas, they'll throw some knives,' and he chuckles.

'No, Kavad,' I say, 'it's you who'll be on the wire. Look on your little screen – they've found a hundred ways to make you hurt. It's bomb and torture time, it makes your flesh creep ...'

'I know, I know,' he cries. 'I'm not a savage, I know Dickens too. The Fat Boy, yes!'

'The web will show the ways to make you shashlik, Kavad,' I say. 'But you can't call the Fat Boy fat – unless he gives permission, or it is a pseudonym for when he sings.'

Kavad has a three-part tic: it makes him twin to Omar. He makes you watch it through, it is a badge, a mark of kingship, maybe, the line long under dust. Twins parted at their birth, sprung from the soil, like Green Men. Dénouement in a final act. 'The real one, please stand up and show a birthmark.' Their faces tic-tocking, till they're tumbled down ...

'Statues, too,' he says.

The face will be clockworked, to show his tic, my *bras armé* tucked under one of his.

'You're rather short, Kavad,' I say. 'You need a horse. A camel. Elephant.'

Then he talks – for hours. How those past wars – they were for identity, nations, languages, religions, all the stuff that's in the past and drowned. Now, it's all commodities. And that's our trade – you can't skim off commodities, for people are commodities as well, and so you trade them too, as wholes, and then they move around, it's always been that way.

'You see,' he says, 'Neanderthals – they were the biggest threat, and now they've gone, assimilated, and yet that struggle still reverberates – Bulgars and Huns, us and those other guys.' He talks and talks. 'I have a mind,' he says, 'that we should all be vegetarians. Not good for the animals, maybe good for us. It is a choice that statesmen make – the many suffer, and the few do too.'

'An elephant is crass,' he says, 'talking of the statues. Unicorns are good, but quite obscure and hard to ride. A camel makes the people laugh, a plinth is glum. And must that leave a horse? No – I have it: on foot, with lions and tigers on a leash, and underneath my arm, your arm. To symbolise that I am arm in arm with all, my friends, my enemies, and those still undecided.' He laughs:

'The new casino – you could stand and welcome them, the punters. "Roll up," I hear you cry, "Inside there's one-armed bandits by the score,"' and then he doubles up, and laughs until I cry – 'Kavad! You bastard – it was all a joke, a pun! To have some fun, at my expense.' I'd hit him and my instinct makes a fist ... The fist is gone, and Kavad says,

'It's pure coincidence, my friend, although the joke's on you. That language is a slippery thing, quite like paternity, you must have heard.'

'My shows?' I ask.

'That sword dance – it's gone on for centuries,' he says. 'And so if Georg's play is any good, it must not change, and it will be a feature permanent. That's is what makes art art, divides it from performance, as your programme notes have said so many times. Permanence, the original, unchanging. He'll do the Priests, the Doctors, Scientists, whatever it is all about, and guys will come from all the world to watch, and play our tables ...'

I say, 'And that way, all the time, the play will change.'

I tell Daria. About how it's now all commodities and credit, about how it's not about identity, but happiness. She says,

'You should be able to take a joke, my dear. People hate those who can't. But now – everyone can do, be, everything or anything. We can't call Georg's stuff The Warriors, The Bankers, whatever comes to mind. We'll call it: The Show.'

'Better still,' I say, 'The Play. And then we'll all be in it, all the time.'

'Don't be a sourpuss, dear,' says Daria. 'Sarcasm is out of place. Mara will do her dance, and sing about the Carmelites, the Bassarids, or Trojans – whatever comes into her head. She is quite specialised, that's true. She'll need her spot.'

'I'd hoped to give it up,' says Mara. 'But if there is a joke involved, I'll do my spins.'

In a shed, there's Kavad, his statue; puffed up in resin – the face, thinking of something else that's surely not identity. The features more spread out than life: it wears a Parthian hat, a smock, and brigand's boots. Some sculptor making compromises. Beneath his arm, my arm. I slide it out. Red moment ... I seize his arm, and break it off. Now, he looks more chipped by life, and solitary – the lions and tigers not yet moulded, cast. I take the clockwork tic, the mechanism set for three contortions. Should it be tweaked to four – like mad Omar's, Anna's twin, now Kavad's twin as well, the second fiddle in the piece? Red moment – another of them. Easy to fix, this automaton. Its movement now is 'perpetuum', producing an eternal squirm, the nods, the winks, the nose that sniffs in triple time, the ears that jiggle up and down, the mouth – that runs from gawp to grin, to slaver, slobber, smug and smirk. I cram the mechanism in his head, set to 'perpetuity'.

'That's justice?' asks Vlad. 'Drawing a moustache, like? Making ridiculous?'

'No, it's happiness,' I say. 'Mine. Just for a moment, between a loss and apprehension. Great satisfaction.'

'And being found out,' says Maas. 'That's not clever.'

'It rather leaves things as they were, but you should watch out, you've one arm left,' Vlad says to me. 'Now, listen – you, down from the stars, and into art and contraband. It's all ephemera, what you do. You barely count. This place is like the other places, the people like the other people, now, before, or in the wings. The rules all over say – although we're poor, we act like rich. The bosses never do the dirty things themselves. Remember too, you never, never, aim for justice till there's no reprisal possible. Happiness, though – you're right. You can fit some in anywhere.'

Mara tells me, 'Now, you're decent, punished – but I must keep my distance from you. You're a cinder.'

'My sweet!' says Daria, joshing with me, laughing in my face, 'It's always so – your fear of reprisal – being castrated – haunts. So every loss – you compensate. What's cut off, becomes an arm. A call to arms, armed struggle – it's so clear ...' and on she rambles, Mara's quite enthralled – my, she'd be a heavy one to lift and hoist aloft: playing along, I say,

'Quiet, Daria – it's all politics, not sex, and not ambition, being liberal and such. I'll show my stump, if you are not convinced,' and there is laughter.

Daria says to me, quite serious, 'You've had your laugh on Kavad. Now you're done for.'

'So are you all,' I say. 'Laugh or not. Kavad's done the bad things, or he's seen you do them all. The innocent, the Maras – they'll all be thrown in, just to make the tale more dark. The cries, the compassion, all stirred in, to make – good story, bad fairy. We're all to go into the pot, the omelette, when the hunger's on him.'

'It's not so,' says Mara, struggling with some tears: she holds my arm, I feel her body down my body's length: 'Not necessarily. You – you once took command, and ordered things.'

'It's not like that,' I say. 'The trouble is – one big god manages the earth, with rules you do in school. But then – the universe – it's like a supermarket, shelves are overfull, or else there's miles of emptiness. You need a host of little gods, and bigger ones that stretch on up the hill, each with her task. They order guys to fill the store, the skies, the universes, and empty out when shelving dates are passed. They get the profit for themselves – if some there is. The rule is:

'fill up the space with sparkling dust, and bag it with some classic name.' But what the purpose is – who knows? You can't eat stars, or emptiness. There are no customers, and we're the weevils in the biscuits. And as for those invisible sky monstrosities – the bear, giraffe, the hunter – and to bring it home, the heavenlies, the twins, what do they signify? ... Kavad doesn't register all this – but, if you are a sceptic, as he is, you get a longer run. Much longer. It's true, composers, choreographers – they get to do the fire and thunder, awe and space. I know, I brought them in – there is a catalogue I use. But ... It isn't real, you understand. When the notes end on the page, it's done. The guys just get their envelopes, and have some drinks. But Kavad can go on, until he's dead, and then he leaves his shoes, his history, for someone else.'

'I hadn't thought,' says Mara. 'That what shoes are of course – history.'

'We'll give you refuge,' Georg says to me. 'Even a role, a part. With one arm – throwing knives is what you do.'

'That's just a circus, it's the same as what Vlad and Maas can do,' I say. 'But theirs is justice. Mine is aiming right, that's all. Everybody knows – dire things that happen to you everywhere: Jim, not a bad man. Waiting for his proof. Zef – who can tell? Let's say we suspect he was quite bad. There's no mathematics in this justice, nor in the being bad. Everybody knows all that.'

'Then, there was Anna,' Georg says. 'While you've been blathering on.'

'I hadn't heard she's dead,' I say. 'She'd put herself beyond us all. A hollow dame, she had become. The furs and gold – it turned you off.'

Anna's death's a mystery, though not to her – too many suspects: better think of something else.

A brown man, all in brown, pulls an ancient brown bear up the street. The bear doesn't know if it should sit or stand. Perhaps it doesn't feel there's difference enough. The guy has furry ragged shoes. He's lucky, he can lace them up. One-armed, I can't do mine. I don't want to end up in a circus, not for justice; nor in Georg's, which is just for fun.

Here's a Chinese delegation: maybe they are missionaries – the last ones brought alphabets, lots of different ones, and trouble. 'No, no,' says a Chinese, 'we're not investing, we're a watercolour class.'

Is this the new? Is it the abyss? A statue here would do, Groucho Marx, bending low, as if the bum's rush was his planned way of departing for his ventures new.

Here come the transhumanists – a congress, and they will leave a hall, full of better beings, all wired up, illuminated. It makes us think of how we could be finer guys, dead eyes a-sparkle, brains without a sin. No cadavers in our sights. Fuck the unadventurous who aren't plugged in. Away! this blundered species, on with the next. Their chief says, 'You're sceptical because you've only got one arm. We can help you: buy another, or – we'll grow you one.'

I'm nonplussed – on the Trans-Siberian, with the trans – there you're free, and you're immortal while the journey lasts. All for love, not sex, and all together, mortal or just what the hell.

'If I'm bionic,' I say. 'It'll just be for me, forever. No one else will care, relate, nor I for them. And maybe I'll be – just an arm. Snapping its fingers in a box, no string to pluck, no hair to smooth.'

'You don't know much about the modern,' says the guy, the transhumanist, to me, not especially kindly. Perpetual motion, he must mean.

Anna. I'd forgotten her death. We should be mourning her. We think of silence, maybe that is right, the tribute. After all, it was in life she made her noise.

'How did they end it for her?' I ask. Mara says,

'Oh, she was quite relieved. It's always the waiting. Like you, waiting for your train. Your Trans,' and she laughs.

'No, no,' I say. 'Not for sex. For love. Like you, Mara. For the idea of love. It's not sex.'

'It's always sex,' she says, 'like it or not. The rest is what you can't have, though it's what you say you want – it's not out there. The little that you have of it, is all there is.'

'No, Mara,' I say, 'it's not about you, it's for Anna. Of course I love her, now, now her house isn't falling on us, and this country – it will be bombed and occupied, and in the ruins after – dawn, or Kavad still. Who can tell? First, the epitaphs – "Rest, rest, my soul, and forget what threatens you." That will do for Anna.'

'It's for you!' says Mara. 'All your bad deeds.'

'Daria's too,' I say eagerly. 'Though I don't know why I'm eager. I don't believe in expiation.'

'Anna just threw herself around,' says Mara. 'From puritan to tart and back again, then down the stairs, her throat bled out, with just one mystery mark. No reason. So, no mystery.'

'We did nothing,' I say. 'Jim, Zef and me, that whole generation, the romantics. The problems start when people love their leaders. When the chief is mean and skimpy, like Kavad there – well, he kicks out, but there's no damage done. What they call the good – is always there, and everybody thinks they have a piece – it's like a stolen host, buried beneath the stoup ...'

'That's crap,' says Mara, 'You guys weren't romantics – opportunists, rather. And burying stuff – it doesn't keep the guys that's after you away, not even if it's cadavers that you've stowed down there outside your house.'

'Enough!' shouts Daria – 'You can't agree, that leaves it all suspended. Small thugs or big – is that the best your argument can gyre around? You simply say the obvious. And wrong.'

Mara says to me, 'Ours is the best relationship, you know. You and me. The end before the start.'

'We've nothing, Mara,' I tell her. 'It's Anna we should miss, some emotion she might have left on us.'

'They washed her,' Mara says. 'She came out white. Just two checkmarks on her neck, as if a snake ... White as the silver on a photograph.'

'A plate,' I say. 'Not the paper, the glass.'

'I don't think you really know,' says Mara. 'White with blue beneath, like sea frozen in an atlas.'

'She was always terribly pale,' says Daria. 'It's the flat frontal light they have here.'

'She was always a bit loopy,' Georg chimes in.

I say, 'I'm not sure that's your right, saying that.'

'I didn't say loopy, I said *loupée*, French,' says Georg. 'Though maybe the one comes from the other.'

'It's transition,' I say. 'The place is flattening out. See the houses, all painted bright. The people, names, religions – no one cares so much. It's a subject you still want to stay away from, anyway. Give Kavad credit for it, if for nothing else.'

'Who can have done it – Anna, I mean,' Mara wonders. 'Maybe it's not relevant.'

Although the cops here are still short guys, they've found some types who stand on guard, extremely tall, so high you know they've not been brigands. There is a zoo as well, though you mustn't call it that. Our horses – gone for pet food, I expect, they eat so much, more as they grow old.

Mara sings:

'In my wooden house, wood skin out and wood skin in,
Snow wrapped outside, dried apples in a glass.
Waiting for you, with everything to give –
The bike with no tires, cat with no bell,
The train halts, you must jump down, take the cold path,
Then caress me, here in my soft warm skin ...'

I ask, 'Why jump down? Isn't there a platform?'

'No,' says Mara. 'But you needn't worry – nothing comes the other way. I don't mean "you" of course. And I'm here, not there.'

'Well, you idiots,' Daria says. 'I brought in circuses. It's the bankers made trouble with the bread.'

'I thought I brought them in,' I say. 'The bankers too – their girls at least.'

'There's too many people die here, without we know what they've done,' says Mara. 'I hope there isn't stacks of them, somewhere in the wood.'

'Things come and go, Mara,' says Daria, brisk and stern. 'There's voices, there's benevolence, there's claims and panic, and there's fiddling. Music. Just do what you can, and wait for judgement.'

Anna in her box, looks like Ophelia. Kavad says, 'I know all that, the play. I'm not a savage. But does she go to church or mosque? She's close to being saint. It's hard to tell.'

We stroll around the town with her, and then we leave her, abandoned in the box, in between religions. Next day, she's gone. 'The wolves took her up the hill,' says Georg, and I say,

'Mara, stand over there, and close your eyes. I ought to practise,' and Vlad comes to watch the knives. I close my eyes as well. My single arm, it

makes me fall a little out of balance, out of line. Still,
I'm very good.

'Things go so bad,' says Daria. 'People are so sad,
they never reconcile.' I say,

'Daria, forget the people, what they think and how
they get on with themselves and all the rest. What
matters is us, how we who run things, how we get on.'
She isn't satisfied: she says,

'I may convert ...'

'Daria – you're crazy! You think of that, when
Mara grieves for Anna, her great love ...'

'She doesn't seem put out,' sniffs Daria. I say,

'People don't show, not like they do in plays.
Mara sang – her house laid out for Anna. Trees with
their silver bark, the silver snow, the silver rails, the
wolves, their yellow eyes ... Anna's house had fallen
down, and Mara, naked at the door, the ice queen
waiting for the train, her precious visitor ...'

'You're crazy too,' says Daria, but I see she likes
the picture, takes her mind off Anna.

'If they'd spirit,' Daria says, 'the guys here'd wire us
up from lampposts, but they wait, they wait.'

'They can't decide,' says Mara, 'and the candidate
for after would be Omar, up there in the hills.

Mourning his sister, who's an asset now she's dead. Besides, these slender lampposts – too tall to tie a cord.'

'I'm out of this,' I say. 'I'm just performing,' and I twirl my blades.

'No, no,' says Daria. 'The idea's this, straight from our genius, our Kavad. We'll put on The Play. With the justice guys, joining Georg's "just-for-fun". Tie them together, and the city will be full of them for years – it is our theme, and let's us out. Justice for everyone, and we're the masters of the scene.'

'It sounds a little obvious,' I say.

'Exactly,' Daria says, 'that's why no one thought of it before. Old-style justice, all in red, and dancing to the bagpipes all the while.'

'And look!' Mara takes me aside and says, 'We could buy a house. I must practise dance. We'd be sister and a brother. Even twins.'

'No,' I say, 'not that. And build, don't buy. Buy, and there's heirs, blowing down your house. And there's other things ... Complicity and guilt.'

'Lesbianism,' laughs Mara. 'It sounds like an ideology that you do at school. It makes no difference, when you're throwing blades. I'll do my *fouettés*. You, reading the Code of Terpsichore, before the fire.' She puts her fetching pusscat's face close up to me. 'You wouldn't have to lift,' she says.

'The Play,' says Vlad, 'it's classic. Us, in league with Georg, sweeping you away, you bastards all, quite indiscriminate, unmourned the lot of you. Georg just having fun, and us with scimitars.'

'Be very very careful,' Daria says to me. 'When they whirl you off – what you wear, the music in your head.'

'I did nothing, Daria,' I say. 'I did it all for art, and there, diving down, in those dark waters you can imagine everything.'

'It's all things supposed, or that happen unwished,' says Mara. 'Do you shovel out the path – maybe a letter comes. If you don't – the things with claws will climb, and down the chimney drop! – baked in the fire – and eat you all. Every scrap. And there you'll be inside. Complicit. Peering from their eyes, scratching their itch.'

'Did you ever get a letter, Mara?' Daria asks, not kindly, 'or even see the mailman? I bet you're still waiting for those beasts.'

Kavad's fixed the tic – not on his face, but on the statue, passed it to the lion, who grins and yawns and sneers. You're supposed to love Kavad – his face a bronze shield, the arm replaced, that welcomes or draws up to swipe. Love, surely without sex, and knowing he is in his place; that reassures. Yesterday will be quite like tomorrow. People don't look at him, but at the lion, it's an attraction.

There's a show – The March on Rome. 'They're singing to the Waste Land songs, even a dance, a bit stiff-legged. Poor men!' says Daria. 'Struggling with their history and their songs and dance. This place is filling up with rich men. What'll we do with them? Where can they be stored? In boxes? What will their countries do without them?'

She looks around the city. Does she take it in? What, if she does?

'No,' she says. 'I shan't convert. No religion has ever lasted for ever. You might want it so. Those poor animals, sacrificed so needlessly. The families cling together round the knife. Did those creatures love their life as I love mine? You can't want what you've had, you don't know what's to come. So – it's just this moment, full of longing and of love, waiting for the miracle. Jim's proof ...'

'Daria, watch out,' shouts Mara. 'Your door is open, and it's flapping in your wind.'

'Kavad today, some guy called Johnstone or Bao tomorrow,' Daria says wisely, with resignation.

'No, Daria,' I say. 'It's just our special state, the feeling vulnerable. For normal people, it's not about the big guys, and their fruits. You suffer, you rejoice, you rampage through the streets. Then, all is changed. You do the proof, you win a prize, more cash than forty donkeys cart away. There is applause. It's not about politics, nor love. It's about the ending up.'

'I think that's crap, my dear,' says Daria. 'All that you say. The puzzle's in your head, there is no prize. Some other guy will spot the proof, for him there is no prize. Or her.'

'That's a philosophy you've got there, Daria,' says Mara enviously. 'I just wait for what comes next.'

'You need a philosophy if you're going in the whirligig,' says Daria. 'They'll put you in it anyway. It's only with democracy you know what's coming next. I'm like you, Mara, I prefer to wait.'

'Hey, you lucky guys,' says one of Kavad's men. 'You're going in the whirligig, the triumphal car. Just wear these boots,' and he hands round those tall Greek actors' boots, for standing tall: 'Who wants a wig?' he asks.

'I'll take a green one,' Mara says.

'I'm ginger,' Daria laughs.

'There's no snipers here,' the guy says. 'We're not yet a democracy. This place is clean.' It's true. There is the photograph, the concert halls, the slippery mound where Omar lives, the statues and the tombs with puffs of flame. 'I'll have a white wig,' I say, 'Not a *mèche*. A big bouffant one, so they'll all know, I bring them in – the dancers, the enforcers, players. I'll put these knives where you can see. And what'll be the animals that whirl us round?'

The guy approves, he says, 'It's great to work with you grandees, that enter in the spirit, in the show. We thought of onagers, but they leap. So it was zebus.'

We're disappointed. Not feisty, those animals, and slow. But there they are, you can't complain.

'Come on!' shouts Daria, 'No one's going to snuff us out – that would be a cosy end – though not so nice for us. No moral messages! No reforming, no "into the light"! On with your wigs and boots! Wherever this place thinks it is, we'll show them, set an example. Into the car, the whirligig, whip up those zebus ...' We can't resist. We wouldn't want to. It's a punishment. To put us on display.

'Do you think the people loves us?' Mara asks. The zebus hardly make it up the hill.

'Don't be foolish, Mara,' Daria says. 'At least they don't do drugs, that way they don't have to go to jail. Find someone, Mara, lay your body right along theirs, dream if you can.'

'If we're in the play,' Mara persists, 'we must have parts.'

'In it, not of it. We just say what we think, we're not the actors with their lines,' says Daria, whipping at the beasts.

'The guys don't understand that, Daria,' I say. 'To them, the show's just unearned punishment. Destinations don't come in for them.'

'To us, the destination matters,' shouts some guy.

'No, it's the legitimacy,' another joins in.

'It's making them responsible ...' another says.

'If we're responsible for something – what then?' I shout.

'Don't answer them,' says Daria. 'It's communication we are after, not answering their questions – each has a different one.'

I think of those iron guys, long ago. Africans, going back to Africa. They knew the principal contradiction, following the path, falling off it sometimes, but always articulate, always the plaster had an iron frame.

'If only I had been like them,' I say. Daria knows about all that, building the pyramids, being infallible, immortal too; the right dynasts. Corrupt.

Now our guys, not content with knowing things, but longing for the mystery – immortality the secret. Capital, they call it now. Instead, just bringing desecrations, like my missing arm, the drawings in the church – cutting down to size.

'No! Don't imagine it!' says Daria. 'It's gone, the past! Not even your fantasy can revive it. Those guys, the iron guys – in bush, savannah, city dump. That's gone, as if it never lived or sat talking till the dawn.'

Kavad must press on, right to the end. All a mistake, I guess.

The zebus reach the top, they see the slope, and break away. Our chariot runs on. The zebus watch awhile, then trot back to the zoo.

The rubber tires send out a 'sol', as we race down the slope. The guys – no horses now to trade – are pecking at their scratch-cards, don't look up. Daria shouts – 'Look, we have been dumped', and some guys stare, as down we go, our wigs flame out, and Mara sings about the Trans-Siberian, and how it stopped outside her door and princes with their leather wings would pause and drink with her, and on she sings, the glorious key of G, and now we see the palace, Kavad's, squared off with canalled water, a hydraulic empire built, the peasants eating rice and goldfish, maybe those blue and yellow frogs, and building temples, though they're now pavilions, for foreigners to take their ease and sell their books and tiny movies fingersize. My! there's the flags of every state, and guys with pompoms on their shoes that strut and pose for snapping, showing off those guns we used to ship in with the fruit and now fly in in tons ...

'Here come the dogs,' shouts Mara, and there's hordes running after us, brown, yellow, black, and white, like galvanised turds, they swarm.

'I thought they'd all been shot,' says Daria. 'These must be immortal,' maybe they are, and there's the buildings, not in ochre now but raspberry and apple green, and mussel blue and pearl.

The gilded moulding's all dropped off. I say, 'If we don't end up bad, it's inconclusive – you can't end in fugue, you must somehow recapitulate,' and Daria says, 'You've learnt so little, all the deaths mean nothing to you,' and I agree they don't, though Anna floating in the lake imperial, the pins from silver brooches stuck in her neck like fangs – yes, she brings a tear.

Down, down we go, that's where they sold the gas for automobiles and now the fuel is air and water; the orchestras are starting up, I hear some guy sing – '*Halt – da liegt ja ein Toter*' – 'There's a dead man lying here.' He must be the finale, but now the players run in alleyways and by the river, now grey with some outflows – here they're doing *Ubu Roi*, and there *The King Goes Forth to France*. Somewhere in his temple, Kavad watches, quite indifferent to content, fat with form.

All could be read in key ironical, but better 'G' and smile – there's the courtroom; once justice came with knives and steel, and now it's burial alive.

Mara says, 'Well, it seems I'm with the good guys,' and she turns to me, 'Just reassure me, and save those knives for entertainment.'

'Naturally.' I say. 'Vlad and Maas are entertainment too – they're good guys, though maybe summary. They left it all to you and chance. Better than that, no one can do,' and Daria joins in,

'And Georg, naturally, too, as good as buttered toast with eggs – it all turns into literature, or at the most, to irony...' She would expound, but then I say,

'Mara, we're all as clean as trout, bowling down the stream – but find a hold, for if we hit ...'

The end is death, of course, the cart, with us dressed up like clowns – it hits, we're tossed like straw men, there's a flash, a lucid blink before we touch our destiny, our tree, our pole, our sculpted stone, conclusion engineered.

Instead—

'Look,' Mara shouts. 'This lever is a brake.' We slow and stop.

There are no birds, but there are slender trees. There's bells and calls to prayer.

The smoke from sausages – it forms a bank, the ropes, the bricks and tiles of roasting stuff – it brings back countryside and herbs crushed underfoot. It seems we are not vegetarians. There's rice.

'The water,' Daria says, 'comes from the river – do you remember Jim? You can't call what he got "his proof"?'

Of course we do remember: and Mara jumps down from the cart, off with her wig, and starts to dance. 'I'm made for this,' she shouts. Around, there's other guys who dance, and living statues, bears, and shamans' drums, and clarinets. It makes you think 'Impressionists', 'Deauville', 'Bosphorus'. Or Chinese exercise, with swords; white dogs with pompoms on their tails.

The menace of a happy crowd, even an indifferent one ... It tells you nothing of itself, its cash, its fear of being hassled off in vans. When you tell about yourself, you must shift the time, the place, even the continent.

Where's Mara gone? And Daria? The dancers? I don't expect I'll see them ever. If justice wanted Daria, it will have to deal with Mara too, poor Mara – throw her back, too small to eat.

I try to hide my missing arm. I'm no one's right-hand man. I try to hide my missing friends.

I'm sure they're safe, I know where they would be. I've the passion of a Robespierre, but I'm his bad twin, not going proudly up the steps – I'm not going underneath the knife, I'd take the train before I'd stand before some judge, and go from boss to bossed.

The Play. It seems it's everything. There's operas and spectacles and walking on the wires – it's like stuff written in a book, where childhood, growing up, being adult, having reckless sex, becomes denatured. It's on the page, or in the tent. It's what the guys all say they want, what makes them laugh, not what they really desire. There's something more. What's left, and not on view, the real Play, might be a racing up and down and being who and what you want to be. Being not yourself, but fleeting something ... what you want to be, becomes at last the person that you are, like everybody else ... them being what they want, and so it turns out you are all the same, in wanting. Racing, rampaging, up and down.

Georg eyes his players, holds a pace-stick.

I say, 'I can't find my friends.'

He says, 'They're sure to be behind the photograph. That's where you Southerners meet up, and plot against each other.'

'Really,' I say. 'I'm not from there. My parents were.'

'Aha!' says Georg. 'A life lurks behind that bland remark. Maybe an ethnotext, they're all the rage. You tell your life, and dress it up. Fine writing, like.'

'Look, Georg,' I say. 'Forget my life, I can't make shape of it. And now, I'd like a word about the shows. I think I'm both a feature with the knives, and boss as well. Imagination seems to fail you, Georg, now you put on scored and scripted stuff. I'd like to see more action, street types, insurrection even.'

'The Street is dead,' says Georg. 'It slowed right down. It's tourists clogged it, and besides, running implies a fall. That free float stuff – well, Mara for one, I had to let her go. She fattened up, I couldn't grasp her – a heavy piece to lift ...'

'It was her dream,' I say. 'She found a train that went the other way, and brought her here. Now, for the moment, she is lost.'

'There's other trains,' says Georg, briskly, 'that go right back.'

I say, 'I might write you some string quartets – you play them while you think of something new to do.'

Mara and Daria – they're not behind the photograph – not yet, at least.

'Go "ask Kavad", that's what they say,' laughs Georg, 'You've been comrades in arms – and now your arm is in the singular.'

I think of all the dead most close to us.

'I spot a kind of malaise on you,' says Georg, peering hard: 'All bad things in the past, at least today. And yet – you churn.'

'It's all this moderation, Georg,' I say. 'Is this it? The best? Of everything? Me – I hate moderation, guys pretend they like each other, drop all the causes that they fought for, like wolves tearing at the lambs ...'

'Those causes – don't they seem ridiculous?' asks Georg, humouring me.

'They didn't bother me at all. I'm from the South,' I say. 'And yet, it isn't natural now. These guys all strolling round and glum, not saying ... Then there's people who're not here, not where they ought to be. Unfinished tales ...'

'No, no,' says Georg. 'That's out of date and out of fashion. Tales must end. The shows are structured thus. The crowds here like it so. And everywhere. They need to know bad things are finished with for ever – or they will be in a year or so. Vlad and Maas – they're doing well ...' and he points to a booth on the square, Vlad with a megaphone, hustling the crowds:

'They finish what they start, that is their show. The only justice that is done is what you see. You pull the ropes and you decide.'

I walk on up the hill. Here's Omar, with his tic and villa. The suspect, rebel, candidate, mad future, crazy past.

'You have a palace here,' I say, remembering the log hut where he took refuge, long ago. He shrugs.

I go on, 'You've almost room for two. If I crouch down, in this attic here, why, I see the town, the trucks ...'

'That's because I cut the trees,' he says. 'Much better so.'

That's true.

There's even room for files.

He says, 'No music, mind, if you live here. It riles me up.'

'Of course,' I say, 'It's in my head. I wouldn't know a way to write it down, mostly I think of something else.'

Everything is stable. The hill does not detach and fall into the town. Omar's mantras are a bore. The guys age, follow their genes, what they were born with, but it's paler now. We don't discuss how different each is from each, we know where that can lead.

RETURN OF THE MASTER

'You see,' says the physicist, 'you take the train, and here I am. That should tell you something about travel. Time, too.'

'My time down there,' I say, 'is nearly up. It's normal now, the everything.'

'It's an illusion, stupid,' says the guy: his eyes are red with staring into stars. 'Remember that guy, writer, set up all the stereotypes. Dickens. Established people good and bad. Did it for evermore. The waifs, the fat, the dull, the evil. No need to go onward – and indeed, that way lay the cliff. You can't go on without a risk. The good, the bad – he fixed it all, you can't dissent. You can't go farther on without a risk. Dickens – he abolished risk.'

'Big risks,' I say. 'We have them here.' I think of the big boss, Kavad. He knew his Dickens well. Not being a savage, that was it.

I say, 'There's been some deaths that's unexplained.'

'They always are,' says my Master, impatient: 'What do you want, an explanation of the explanation? The world – is something you can't justify. It's not about some agency. It's process. Greater good, all that.'

He asks, but I'm indifferent to journeying in the cosmos. We leave the veil, the membrane, slack in place.

He peers at my body: 'You're asymmetrical.' I say,

'I used to be mediocre among the two-armed. Now I'm near the top of the mutilated.'

'It won't work,' says the old predator. 'There has to be two. Or indeterminacy. You're definitely a one. You don't fit the plan, God's will. Two by two, man and woman, nostrils, ears and ovaries. It's two. Or dither. Scamper. Never one.'

'One plan, one will,' I say, quick to catch on. 'Besides, mine's a war wound. Settling accounts.'

'What did you learn there?' he asks. 'Did you do a proof?'

'Like Jim's proof? What's the point of a puzzle if there is a proof?' I ask. 'Buy a monkey in a cage. Keep it close by you. Nurture should mean it grows into a man.'

'Then you'd need a bigger cage,' he says.

'I think I'd better travel some,' I say, 'Maybe to a place that I don't know.'

'They're all like that,' he laughs. 'But made up of the same, the twirly loops of twine. String theory, all in unison. It's mystery and proof, all tied in one.'

AFRICA

'How's the music here?' I ask. That's what I've come about. Back to where those iron men, our Africans, originated.

'Just drumming, against the sorcery,' says a guy. 'That's why people come – to drum, or to be exorcised.'

'That sounds just right,' I say. 'And here they've barely finished with a war, so it's like other places.'

We talk, this guy and I, not long enough to see if he is good or bad.

Being poor – you associate with money, or no money. Here, they don't aspire to cash. They can't imagine anything they do would turn to coin and note. They're right. They barter, pound some food, complain, and undergo the evil eye. At least they're penniless. They don't have things you'd want to steal, or borrow.

Their music – is just sticks on logs. Back home, it wouldn't sell.

The big thing here's the evil eye. The ugly ones are bearers, it would seem, the others, symmetrical, their lovely bodies briefly optimal – they've scrawled all over them, to keep the bad stuff out.

I lean against a tree. I take out Kavad's tract, 'On Transition'. The tree has large brown pods. If you were lively, you might harvest them, and crunch them into crispy food. His book says:

Free, or good? Which do you want to be? You may have read you can be both. That's wrong. You can't be either, and you cannot choose. I am a boss, and everyone, including you, who wants to be a boss thinks they'd be free, and could be good – if no one else was. It's not true. I'm not good. Nor am I particularly free.

This is a tract on our transition. Usually that's about some economic trend. Those happen anyway. This, instead, is all about myself. Free? you guys, your women too – you're shackled by your thoughts, and once in a while you'll maybe think of 'free'. But being it? Or being good and going on, whatever happens, being good as good, and no one knows, and even you aren't sure of what it means? No, guys – forget the being good.

It's problematic. Things fall down; they conscript
you, they eat your goats. Forget it. As for being
free – you're only free if everyone is free. It's the
paradox. Forget now what that means, just think –
your kids, your women, doing what they want? Is
that your wish? Just think again – free and
wanting to be free – they're not the same.

*It's hot here, and I doze. Kavad like all the rest wants
justification – that starts off like it's going to be some
justice, but it wriggles, becomes something else ... As
the astroman, my mentor said, nothing that is can be
justified...*

*Oh no! I wake and scream, those goddam pods –
they're living things that suck and suck, they look at
you with pinkish eyes, and suck and watch ... There's
laughter, the locals pick me up, and tell me how the
pods are live, they're creatures napping, just like me,
then waking up to suck.*

*I'm alive. But how pale I am. The pods waddle
away, full of my blood. How hard it is, with just one
arm, to hold a tract and turn a page. It goes on,*

The good – conformity, obedience, my friends!
Freedom – what all the others do – they vote, and
in the end agree. The rest – is scraps. You paint
your house a purple – next door, it's green. If that

144

is 'free' – go ahead! It's all conformity, obedience to the rest, it's craven. Obedience to the rest in time becomes obedience to yourself: surrender, cowardice. They call it solipsistic. Of course, I respect your various beliefs, religions, countries, everything. It means I am indifferent to all, and all the details that you say is good and free, and prize, and set a value on.

It's inconclusive, you will say. It's true. It's inconclusive, just like you. You don't, you can't, conclude. You ought to go beyond – the free, the good. Of course you won't ...

Some blood – it must be mine – is left, and drops upon the page. What did I seek here? Not the drums, they're in the catalogue, they would come when called. Time out of moving right along, perhaps? A stasis. Instead, my bloodletting.

It's clear that Kavad wants to stay and stay – like Omar, Daria. That's the aim. Remain. For ever, till it stops. Transition means what happens after him. Only Mara – lifts, lofts, like a birchleaf in the storm, twisting green on greyish green, as the breeze comes, knowing she won't remain, or propagate, or finish up her dance.

Well, that's too bad for her. That story's hers. Mine's different. I'm not surviving here. Down I go.

There's someone – says, 'Chew on this stick.'

'I should feel lighter, without all that blood,' I say, 'But in fact, I don't.'

The guy says, 'You must seek a sorcerer. This stick helps you hallucinate. I'm into techno; when you chew this bark, it helps a lot with that.'

I say weakly, 'Back where I've come from, people were entranced by gangsta, but I think that's all gone down. Those musics – they were real transition. Not like the Tract; that's about the bosses staying on.'

'It's too bad we can't chat things over when you're better,' says the guy. 'For now, just keep on chewing. When the sorcerer comes, the stick will take away the taste of what he gives ...'

It must be Juan that's talking, he comes in moments of high stress.

The sorcerer's brew is sticky sweet. It's a Manhattan, so it seems. When he's drummed, the wizard talks and talks. He wears a suit, carries a Gladstone too.

'Forget the nature–nurture stuff,' I say. 'Just do the cure, and quick – and let no animals be sacrificed or hassled while it's done.'

He seems offended, 'In a hospital,' he says. 'You'd stay for days and not be diagnosed. I do things quick. This evil eye originates from way back home. It's quite a stubborn thing,' and on he talks.

'I don't think your music travels,' I say, and the sorcerer ignores me. Juan pays him, but not with animals.

'There,' says Juan, fading away. 'Your acute case of evil eye has dropped into the chronic. Here, you had the truth. Not to sleep under pods in trees – is just the start of it. The magic's in the word "transition", and remember too, that nature isn't nurture just for you, but for the pods. It's pharmakon, it kills you if you take too much, cures if you never have enough. It's like the pitcher of Manhattans that you drank. The buzz is for the doctor, not for you.'

His words grow fainter: my good sense returns. I'm left with most of Africa around, and not a drumming act to sign. No iron men, become corrupt. These ghosts are not the past – they're future. Not free, nor good.

Juan, now – he's a good sort. Just once I should take his advice. He really should exist. Since that's not so, I seek out the sorcerer again.

'You keep a fine bar,' I say.

He pours himself three fingers: 'You can't go and fucking die at thirty,' he says, censoriously, 'You have to do the whole trip. You've paid for your ticket. Sit there till it slows. Use incantations, if you must – but to

147

*be redeemer, that's what you must do. Then you'll see
transition. Or you would, if you were there.'*

*I say, 'I'd hate to play redeemer. My physicist –
we travel through the cosmos, watch the blips and
bangs. Do you think we could redeem? It's the dead
who cast the evil eye – you can't do much about that.'*

*He pushes a full dirty glass at me: 'Drink this.
Grow wiser, like I do.'*

*After a while, he says, 'Not spiritual stuff, of
course. That redemption's techno. It lasts till the
power goes off. I'm a doctor. Go back to the people
you have left. Sort all that out.' I ask,*

*'You mean – do something for the guys? The
mass? To tell the truth, we don't think about them
much. So long's they have their work. Besides, they're
all minorities. Clubbing each other with their faiths.
We just think of staying in our saddles – us horsemen
with the long scythes, batting at the guy, our comrade,
who rides alongside ...'*

He hums and incants – 'Einst hielt ich ... *the drink
of freedom, Held high the amethyst beaker,
tumtetum...'*

*I say, tiring of this traditional hospital, its smell
of wriggling roots and viscera – 'I prefer the starry
heavens,' but he holds me back: 'Fiction ought to be
stranger than truth. Truth – you can always look it up*

somewhere. But sometimes there's something stranger than both truth and fiction ...'

My old physicist said the same: 'What do they expect to find, for all that cash, further and further, peeking into those unimaginable distances, the seas of acid, planets made of bones? There's something at the edge. I'm sure it isn't paradise, or someone would be back, thrown out for drink or pederasty. No, someone knows that when you reach the edge there is another edge ...' I used to interrupt – 'Maybe that first lost love?'

'Ah yes,' he said. 'Or else the last,' he made a grin, he's Nosferatu scrabbling up the slope, profanation in his skyblue eye.

I feel rejected, but not unhappy about it. Down from the stars. Escape – from distances, and falling off the edge, and those long claws of his.

'Farewell, reluctant traveller,' the sorcerer says, 'No doubt I'll be around.'

* * *

'Well, well,' says Mara, when my train gets in: 'The gang's all here. At last.'

'Dear Mara,' I say. 'I'd hoped not to be back. Who's in and out, and which am I?'

'Those shows you put on,' Mara says. 'They must be quite important. They're our fresh face to the world.'

'So, well, how's the boss?' I ask.

'At his window, looking in at yours,' she says. 'Benevolence and cleanliness. He hasn't other things to think of. Cleaning up the mud – that's what takes the time.'

'There's no savages left,' I say: 'So I didn't sign the drummers.'

'Vlad and Maas say there's no choices to be made, save in the real,' says Mara. 'That's what touches. The music and the acting doesn't count. And so, they've changed their act. They now sell figurines. Famous figures – you just make your choice, and take them home. The lesson's there.'

'Who needs lessons, Mara?' I ask. 'No savages there are – but I want savagery in my acts. You've no choices when you sit. You could walk out, I guess. No savages, but lots of savagery. That's what we want. Vlad and Maas – were into killing guys by chance, by choice. They should have stuck to that. It gives you hope.'

She perseveres, 'No, no, the choice is like – you pick Penelope, Pascal, or Pétain. Anyone. That is your choice. The working through comes after.'

I say, 'They must have quite large stocks.'

She says, 'You're very pale.' I say,

'My choice of tree was poor.'

Hedging your bets – Pascal, Pétain. Corrupt? Disastrous? Prudent? Penelope, the tease – leading those suitors to the slaughterhouse.

I say to Mara, 'You know, I don't hedge anything. Our cash comes from the traffic, that you see outside ... Where does yours come from, Mara?'

'Well, my friend,' she says, twisting her body into question marks – 'I'd rather hoped ... you being loaded...'

'Sex is a thin glue, Mara,' I say. 'What can you sell?'

'Everything is normal here – I don't want that kind of fate,' she says: 'There's ministries and views. It's all skimmed down, it's watered milk.'

We consider our futures.

Mara says, 'Those sorcerers – they could have conjured up some cash, for everyone.'

'You would have thought so,' I say. 'It doesn't seem to work like that.'

Georg's still into spontaneity: his show will run –
that's all his actors do, they run. He says, 'The thing is
not to be afraid. Just think. You're frightening to other
people. You bore the upper crust – no problem, drill
on, there's crusts and crusties down and down. I'm
quite beyond aesthetics now.'

'That's better so,' I say.

Daria says to me, 'You're in luck now – you won't be
killed. Just put on trial. Of course, that's if he should
decide he doesn't like you.' She laughs, she's gay.
She's been confirmed in second class. They've made a
figurine of her. She says, 'Too bad you lost your arm –
I could have gone as Venus, but put alongside you, we
would look like freaks.'

She stares, like I'm her pot of gold. She says,
'Those people that you killed. I'll keep it quiet for
now, but it will all come out.'

That is one future, certainly.

Then, Omar says,

'This calm! Doesn't it get to you? I feel so angry –
the guys should be swirling in the streets, not in some
play, some spectacle, but smashing things, and
shouting, sharp noses pointed to the sky, and howls! A

mass of them, and me, or someone like me, pushing them, heaving their weight along.'

'Don't pull me down with you,' I say. He waves me aside:

'Anna, she was a stray,' he says. 'She had the passion, not the focus. So – in the end, she got it in the neck.'

'That was another mystery,' I say. 'You and she were lovers, brother and sister, so I always thought.'

'Sister, lover. The labels don't stick to her,' he says, 'Now she's boxed up, and away.'

'I feel it's all precarious. We shouldn't bring our attachments, our sentiments, along. Our life's at stake, where would our loves come in?' I ask.

'That's your nobility,' says Omar. 'It's good when it pops out. It doesn't make you a good tenant, of course. Now – Mara: she's a waif. You take her in – she nips, she fastens on.'

'Don't touch her, Omar. You'll do for her, or else she'll be a sacrifice upon your tomb. Not what she wants, in either case.'

'Oh, she could be the tragic slave, abandoned, loyal and doomed,' he says, offhanded.

'I ought to bring those ancient operas here – it seems your life's in tune with them,' I say.

Omar ignores this: he says, 'I'll need your guys, your soldiers, naturally.'

'I don't have guys,' I say. He ignores this too: he says,

'In the past, when there'd been revolution, we could promise folk another one. Now, our boss, Kavad, is cleaning up. Before he cleans us too, we must think of cleaning cleaner.'

'My guys are happy, doing what they do,' I say.

I say to Mara, 'Don't climb on to Omar's truck.' She says,

'We have to go with him. Though it's the wrong time, and he's the wrong person. We should forget where we are ...'

'And who we are,' I say. 'Mara – the starry heavens are far far off. It's not the right time.'

'Exactly,' she says. 'It never is. That's why we must. Some trains you have to catch.'

'That's so,' I say.

There's the station. I hold her with my arm – she struggles, but she's on the train.

'No,' she shouts. 'I don't want this, not back, not to the steppe. I'll miss my history. This way, I shan't be in the book, the one about the master.'

I'm determined. There may not be more trains that leave. I hold her till it moves, then jump – with one arm, it's less complicated.

Daria says to me, 'You cheated with the house. It all started so. You're a Southerner – you don't grasp aspirations. The guys here – some take the risks, to be together, suffer, make mistakes ... you wouldn't understand all that. And others – striving upwards ...'

'It's true,' I say. 'I'm compromised. I guess with you, it doesn't count.'

'No, of course not,' says Daria. 'Why should it?'

The music, the spectacles, don't seem relevant now – why should they be? Daria, uncaring about what she's done or planned, she hits at me, those big arms like clubs they use for pounding corn. I shout,

'Daria, I can't defend myself. And – I'm a hero. Mara's left, she's safe.'

Daria shouts, 'She's always safe, you fool! That's why she wanted risk! The guys here ...' and I'm sure she'd go on – adding on the Russians, Americans, Europeans too, all flocking in, faces in the clouds, staring down, and contemplating lightning. Chinese too.

I said to my old astrophysicist, as we flew beyond our galaxy – 'It must be risky here, we are the only ones who fly this far, farewell to gravity. We don't know what this web is made of. What if our feet go through, the thing unravels? Or it's sticky, and we're wrapped for ever like dead flies – look! here's an end, and if I pull on it, the string is tied to string, the whole lot pulls apart ...'

'Well, it would happen anyway,' he says, and laughs, and shows his teeth, all well aligned, some white, some black. 'It's all string theory,' he shouts, it's string quartets, trios, probably it's everything – we glide, like fruit bats seeking honey in the stardust, and I think *Enough of the avant garde. What people want's a musical, that's where they see their fragile lives dressed up and sparkling.*

There's mutiny, betrayal. The masses move like treacle, and we masters – we strike each other with our instruments.

I say to Daria, 'Once again, we're a quartet – there's Mara, on the train, Omar who leads his troops and probably the cops as well, and you, and I. There's only Jim and Anna looking on ... It's not about the arts, or politics – just bodies without life.'

You can't hear the music that we make. Mara may be crying, as she sees the birch trees.

Omar now unrecognisable, helmeted, with knee pads.

'What's this about, Daria?' I ask. 'Your career? Some angry guys? This kind of Balkan place denying geography, spitting out its history?'

'No,' she says. 'Jim was a stickler. Anna was a flirt. That's it. It's not responsibilities, it's how the story goes. I'm still in the game. You're not conclusive.'

'That doesn't seem an explanation,' I say, 'of anything.'

'You should have let Mara have your gun. Whoever wants one, that's what you must do. It's the courageous thing. Denouncing Omar too ...' Daria says.

'And me?' I ask. 'Into the streets? Finding the right side? You know, I didn't invent all this, the music – comes from catalogues, the players too.'

'Music is irrelevant, so is all the mumming you've brought in,' she says, and hits with better aim, more power.

I back away, 'I must do what you say? Follow the general will – it's most attractive,' and I point below, down to the guys and cops, the line dance. No guns just now. Shoulder to shoulder, there's the minorities, the fractures healed. I wonder if they know our names, and where we live. My files ... my room in Omar's place ... I say,

'Daria – all your crimes? Do you want punishment or forgetfulness?'

'You fallen star!' she screams at me. 'The deaths, the people trafficked, your complicity ...'

'No guns,' I say. 'And complicity is what we're born with.'

'You're not my judge,' she shrieks.

'If not me, then who?' I ask. 'I know how Anna riled you up. And Jim, and Zef – you were provoked. There's scarcely any blame. Don't cry, I understand you, Daria.'

'You floating dreg,' she shouts at me. 'I cry – it's tear gas! Maybe you're not susceptible to that. It proves my case. You running dog! Two-timer!'

Mara comes in, she's crying too. 'I couldn't get away,' she says. 'I didn't have my passport.'

No jokes about the Trans – right now, it would be in bad taste.

'Mara, this guy,' Daria says, pointing at me with some scorn, 'will show you how to use your gun.'

There's usual action in the road. Wholesalers going for the pills, there's scooters up and down, making a noise like cracking nuts. If the state is failing here, the rest is going well.

I should move on.

My old explorer of the cosmos says, 'It's all for territory – hold it, grab it. Though what Alessia wanted – I can't think. She wasn't Jewish, but she took her gun, and out she went, we don't know where, or even if she had in mind a plan.

'Guys shoot the rockets up – some come right down, covered in germs and spatial fleas. Poor Laika – he had lost his land. Everybody's going back – to caliphs and emperors, viziers, prophets in their trees, everyone is starting over, old-time enthusiasm ... but you must be very very careful. Go too far back, you're with the lizards. Go back just right, to make a better start – the scene just hums with magic; tendrils round your feet, ripe apples at your lips, mimosa in your hair.

You think it starts with steam power, no! It's with obedience and destiny.

'Me – I feel the death that's curdling my bones. I'll try that trick of being dead and yet alive, out in some distant unobservable place.'

He snaps his finger joints, his nails are black and yellow. We share the vision – refugees, their riches in a bundle on their heads, plod along asphalted roads. You see,' he says, 'the roads! That's what they got without appreciating them. Macadam! Unique – those wonderful Scots!'

I have a revelation. 'You're getting round to it – Alessia is looking to restore Laika's turf? His run, his province?'

'Yes, my dear apostle,' the magus says, delightedly. 'Vengeance: the truth. The guys are fighting, all of them, to keep their truth – not freedom, not the right. And no one says what it is they really want, that they have lost, or they can't have. It's territory, with the precious stuff that lies beneath the scrub, the bush.'

'Don't be so rash,' I say. 'It's maybe something more, and different, they seek.' We pause.

I say, 'Perhaps events are not definitive. Maybe there were lots of Laikas. Just for practice.' It comforts me, although I don't like dogs. Nostalgia for the present – he feels it, I do too.

'Yes,' he says, 'They're all there somewhere, seeming dead but all alive, guys shooting up those dogs and having them come down. That was communism – I was one of them, of course, a scientist. In those days the word was concreteness. Not transparency. Transparency's no good. For that, you need a telescope. Just trusting what you see – you'll never spot the lies. Now, what about you? You've got your share of the obsessed – Omar, Kavad, men without a vision. What is yours?'

'Well,' I begin, 'mostly, when it comes to governance, our technique is known as rafting. Surfing, you could call it. Planing on the surface.'

'Ah yes,' says the scientist, 'like Genghiz. Once all Mongolia was covered with the sea. Still trying communism, still shooting up those dogs,' he rhapsodises, he rambles: 'Those days, it was belief in science. They should have stuck to communism. Or maybe it's the belief in belief itself that's wrong.'

'Now you're talking!' I shout out. 'That's something that I recognise. Our resource – it's people. They go on when all the rest has been dug up, piped off.'

That's all? That's quite banal.

'Listen,' says the man of the stars, my master: 'You may be bright, but you're not brilliant – not that the bright ones don't finish in the cellar too. That goddam dog. You really think they were so stupid, they'd sell you cigarettes in memory of a dog burned up in space? "Laika" means a sledding dog, a husky type, just any one. You got it wrong. Again.'

I'm humiliated. I say, 'What was its name, then? Lada? Something like?'

He can't remember. He says, 'My problems are mine, I set them up myself. I can't answer yours.'

It's true, that death in this small universe is threatening him. I think, 'Shove off, then, Master.'

'I must explore,' he says, gesturing a parting of curtains, pretending that he scans the void, 'And find a suitable, a comfortable resting place. If only I could have written it all down – the voyages, the animals. Surfing with prudence since – they poop, especially the bear; and the giraffe – they poop firecrackers!' And he winks, to show it's his extravagance.

I ought to leave.

But I go back.

Art is the footprint of the species, so they say. That is my task, to plant my feet. Our defects are but specks of dust, when you compare them to the clods of shale that larger states throw out – and justify as best they can. Our dirty business is our own, our task, or done by hiring guys in greater need. Then, there is art, eternal. The work I do.

Mara says, 'I hope you're not one of those predators we read about. Is the big change, the transition, at the door? The big Boss, sits in his chair, quite mummified, what must be done is done. It's all in self-defence. Now, Daria's the only interesting one. All she does, is done for her alone.'

'It's true,' says Daria. 'I am the interesting one. But don't you pry!'

I tell Mara, 'People remember the skewers – the weapons; did for Jim, Zef, and Anna. They think those three fall in the same suit: jack, king, queen – all the same, a trio, bound together. They forget the rest, the many – all going off to space in different ways. It's like how you remember, in the movies, not the plot, the stars, but the production values – the colours, the movement of the camera eye, it dwells on that red railing, those pretzels in the bowl, the wonder that they make. Bad acting sets it off, quite brilliant. That's what you remember.'

'That's what I want,' says Mara, sidling close, 'to be a star. That was my destiny, not to be the hat-check girl. You know about the stars – so, you can make me one.'

'I bring them in, the stars, it's true. I have a list of them. And some remain, unseen by day, but when there's justice needing done, or lighting up this urban scene – why, out they come. But Mara – you must know, I had a girl, Alessia, she took her gun, and disappeared. Dog-soldier. Dog star, unfaithful hound,' and on I go, poor Mara, there's her wooden house, propped in the tundra, maybe on the edge there's taiga, and the trains that weekly pass and some will stop, and some will crack ... where Mara dreams to be a star.

'Mara,' I say, 'we have to fight, perhaps, before surrender is inevitable. You fight or flee – in the long term, it doesn't count. You usually do both.'

'We have to save our skins,' adds Daria, 'I've so much of it, too. Order. Riches, satisfaction – keeping the faith. We don't want that, not any of it. Right, you two? Up there, the starry heavens, down here, the painful compromise. The probability of error. We don't want that, Mara. Nor that other guy's ideas – equality, consensus – living as a species should; instinctive democrats!' She makes a snarl. She has a camel's lips.

We have artists in residence, of course. Arbitrary justice, and complete licence – as you would expect, and hope. Vlad, Maas, Georg.

Daria says,

'The point, Mara is this: everyone who can decide is unworthy. Stained. But there it is ...' and Mara interrupts, 'I'm not an innocent, you know.'

'Of course not,' Daria says, as if she's reading off a machine: 'It's just that I have a throne, but I've no palace. All of us with thrones want palaces. In this town, we have one, with a paddy field, embodying our linkage with the East. That palace is occupied. And then there is the prophet on his slide, Omar, without a throne or palace. Does he have a vision, or is it just psychosis? I was so close to him ...' and she shudders at the memory. Maybe it's a shiver.

'Daria,' I say, 'you want our guys to fight for this – do you call it an idea?'

'I'm not making points,' she says, 'I'm navigating. My husband, pacifist, benevolent – we should make a statue for him, for he showed the way ...'

'Oh no!' I shout, 'spare us the ribbons and the doves.'

'Well,' she says, 'the guys here, rebels and the rest, are paid to get beat up. We'll leave our images behind, like when we did the whirligig. A great mistake that, though we'd little choice. We made our mark in memory, did the show – and lost our auras when the cart went down ...'

How banal this is, and Mara quivering there, she's got her gun, just like Alessia, ready to go beyond the stars. But – she's an actress, maybe this doesn't count.

Mara says, 'That's a founding myth all right. All the elements are there. That's no comfort, though – there's nothing I could have done. Down from the stars you came, back the survivors go – up to the stars. And Anna? A mystery.'

'Oh not at all,' says Daria, who's taken with the idea that we have set things up, can disappear, safe and silent: 'Anna tied her choker tight, and the fangs, her brooch, entered in her blood. It happens frequently. She was an Egyptian queen, for sure, and lovers, well, a disappointment always, even if they spring from convenience, a *raison d'état.*'

Alessia the hunter – the Master warned against desires for settlement out there in space. Better to be a constellation than bet upon a single star, its red, its blue. I'm not so sure. The good, the equitable, the true – what resolution do we leave? There's always looking for the true, and hope it's somewhere written down.

'Besides,' says Daria, 'Mara should realise, we're not all stars. Think of that Rogers girl, and Fred Astaire, dragging her through those dance routines. Poor girl, she couldn't keep the time, they put putty on her claquettes to keep her quiet. And yet – her name is chained to his, his irritation burning into hatred as she let him down ...'

'I can't follow this,' says Mara, through the tears, 'I am the dancer, after all, and none of you can spin or twist...'

'Enough!' says Daria. 'Death threatens all of us. You too Mara.'

Mara shouts, 'Fuck you! I'll set the wolves against your forests, the burning brands tied to their tails ...'

Daria says, 'No, Mara, not wolves, that was foxes.'

'See if Alessia shoots them, then – she's just a constellation, so you say,' screams Mara.

It's true – every time I look up in the sky, I think of her, Alessia. Memory, no more.

Mara's no patsy – look, she takes her vengeance. The fire is written in the record – see the minarets, the steeples, burn, the forests have long gone, but everywhere there's logs. There goes Omar's house, that's also mine; the central palace doesn't burn, of course, surrounded by its moat.

The idea? It can't be that: – regime after regime, show after show... you get them from the catalog, off with the old, the useless, faster, faster ... No, we must be kept safe, something must be solid, not ephemeral, not the material, withering. Not the real, already losing muscle tone, rotting fast ... There must be refuge, a haven we believe in, even as we prepare our flight.

It burns, Mara's fire, burns like a star. Not the concrete – the concreteness – of course, which cannot burn. The Master tried to say what happens when a star burns up – not quietly burning out, for it's a gassy fire, but something's left; it should be cold, out there so far and on its own. It sounds like opera – but there's no curtain call.

'Dialectics,' the old guy said. 'That's what's left. Not stars, not matter, not the real.'

'Anna was vendetta,' Daria says.

We watch the blaze – she doesn't explain, neither the fire, nor Anna's end.

'We must survive,' I say. 'There's still a palace politics that we might save, and might save us,' and Daria laughs, and says it seems those pills my people trade now have pronounced my ultimate, defining word.

'Pills are for happiness,' I say.

'It's not the time,' says Daria, 'for you to have hallucinations. Here is the truth about our friend, our Anna. Anna wasn't part of it, of us, of anything. She's somewhere in between the start and finish. That's what vendetta is. The chain that binds us all together.' That doesn't make much sense.

'Maybe I went too far,' Daria reflects, 'with Mara. You never know what mousy girls will do, when you provoke. Meanwhile, I've lots of organising out in front of me. At least, some bags to pack. I'm irritated – I only say the truth – people resent it – and you see! Arson. Is what happens.'

There's flares of purple, scours of red within, like peacocks' tails, the fire more lively than the blocks and towers it eats.

'No doubt my judge would be that Vlad,' says Daria. 'Goddam day I brought him in. Justice is not the way. It is a blunderbuss. Mara should have stayed back there, entertaining the trans that throng the trains ...' and she laughs at her little play. I can't pursue her calculations and her gyres. I hear her, but I think of something else.

'Alessia is fine,' I say. 'She was promoted, all can see her constellation now, tranquil when it's cloudless, they say her gun looks like a bow ...'

'Come on,' says Daria, impatiently. 'No fancies now. You've no idea where Alessia went, or why.'

The Master goes voyaging up there – or is it down there – maybe he knows. Maybe he sees Alessia.

'Don't gawp, you two,' shouts Daria. 'Mara, you're in disgrace. You've ruined us and saved us – although that is the best. Life here is wobbling. After us comes something else. No time to speculate right now. We leave a layer of black ash, survivors puzzle over it for centuries, they always do. Now, do we resist? Or take our cash and settle somewhere else?'

Mara's tearful once again: 'I've got no cash,' she sobs.

I say, 'Mine all went on art. Justice and freedom, that was it, and costly too.'

My old friend Juan's by me, and he knows I'm not the kind who dies in battle and then waits to be informed what for. 'Forget historians, in the species' name,' he says. 'Save yourself, and take your stash ...'

'My stash was buried on the hill,' I whisper to him. 'Now there's confusion – foreigners around and seeking fortunes, come to see the show; the hill is black, consumed, and tumbling down. My stash is somewhere underneath.'

Juan has gone; if he had hands, he'd throw them up, despair.

Now Mara says, 'We'd better all be brought to trial, the good, the bad – justice demands ...' and Daria shouts,

'A trial? Those criminals? In judgement over me? The massacres they did, and now they want to polish off the scene – trombones and cymbals! Mara, forget the string quartets, and thinking of some other, some more pleasant things. This is the earthquake – away,

away from habitation, things that drop, ceilings and beams!'

'I have a good idea,' I say. 'Quite odourless. It leaves us on the winning side, whichever that will be.'

'Oh no,' says Mara. 'Not in the cart again. No, no, I won't go.' I explain—

'The three of us will represent Kant, Rousseau, Marx. Each had his feminine side, it doesn't matter which of us is which. White coats or togas, Daria? Which animals to draw us, Mara?'

We'll be a reasonable doubt, conformity, and hope. Of course, we leave the subtlety aside.

The zoo is almost empty – the little animals gone as pets or roasts, the big ones wishing they were small.

'Draught animals don't have to come in pairs,' says Daria, as though she knows.

'Together, we three wise men, with those values, we're compatible with all religions here,' I say to Mara, 'and keep your gun as well.'

We take two oxen, white. Humble beasts, they're moping in a field. They don't look happy. Mara says,

'Must we whip them? How is their acceleration?'

'Mara,' Daria shouts, 'don't act bewildered. You don't whip oxen – there are goads. This one's electric – old one-arm here, he can have that one,' and she thrusts it at me, she had goads tucked in her 24-hour case, she'd thought of everything.

She says to Mara, 'No one will truck you off and kill you, drop you from helicopters, into quicklime, or have their fun with you before they tire. At least, it is improbable. Straighten up, young Mara. No Trans-Siberian train will pass, no trans get on or off. You're with us now – you're a philosopher ... think, don't tremble so.'

Her words inspire. The cart moves off, the oxen look as if its movement's new to them. Our brows are girt with laurel green, we bob, and blow a kiss to those who stare.

'Look, Mara,' I say, 'the moving statues. We invented them. They are unique. They tic, they toc.'

'I see them,' she says.

Georg's players stop their act, and stand stock still and stare at us.

'We're the good guys,' Daria says. 'It's always been a quiet place here. No genocides, no persecutions, no one trucked away.'

We have the philosophy with us, on our side – all kinds. Most people recognise it.

'What did you want, Mara,' Daria asks. 'Love? Movement? You can't get it off of him,' she laughs and points at me. 'He's only got one arm. You should have stayed and waited for your train. The trans gives love. That's the profession.'

'I never understood why he gave – why they took – his arm,' says Mara.

'Well,' says Daria, 'his love, Alessia, she's in the sky, or underneath us. As for his arm, do you suppose he made a sacrifice? An obligation? I think for once – he was a bad bad boy, and not for love! Did you know, Mara, the Earth's not flat, though usually it's helpful to see it so. Nor is it round – it has a curve that moves with you. Not an edge, you understand – a curve that's always there, but one you never reach. Revenge. A destiny. Settling life's accounts. Puzzle it out! That should explain Alessia – maybe it explains you too.'

Here, there's stuff that's burnt and dead, but some new towers sprout up. There's guys who see us pass, they stare, they do not stop.

This crap about the round, the flat, the curve – the Master would have laughed. The curve is everywhere – it's not a horizon, like the birds, or ships, are first invisible behind, then – here they are! No, as he says, even nothing has its curve.

'Mara,' I say, 'being without an arm – it doesn't make me happy, if that is what you think. The people here – they're not happy, however many arms they have. I covered them with music, quartets, voices, everything. And sure, that way makes you happy, though you cannot always tell. And not for long.'

The guys are in the paddy fields – they're not too happy either.

Mara says, 'That stuff is not to eat. They make it into gasoline.'

'We should have been the Left,' I say, 'but that takes lots of capital. I remember Lenin said it – what a disaster for us if those rich countries don't join in.'

Daria scans to right and left: she says to me,

'You're crazy – the idea of taking us all back to Africa to put some metal in our bones ...' She sighs, 'Anna was the best of us.'

'That's maudlin, Daria,' I say. 'Africa never was the place for us.'

'Maybe I just don't want to meet with Jim again,' she says.

'Now, that's talking, Daria!' I say. 'I don't much want to see the starman either, though he's alive and crawling somewhere in the sky. As for Alessia – I'm not so sure we're made for long relationships, at least, not with each other.'

'I love to hear that talk of Lenin,' Mara says. 'My grannie had a picture of him.'

'So did everybody's gran,' says Daria. 'Just concentrate on steering straight.'

A swarm of cellists, bright wingcases strapped on to their backs, climbs on the train. 'They never got to play,' I say. 'When they are running hot, it's hard to think of other things.'

'Yes,' Daria says, 'you brought the culture in. Just think, at the beginning there was just that dance with swords. Humiliating for the losers.'

The oxen tire.

There's mixed reaction from the crowds, and some throw stones.

'My friends,' says Daria to us, while ducking down, 'forget philosophy, but – if we don't go back, we'll never know what happened in the palace, who won, and occupied.'

I say, 'Kavad is sad, and Omar's mad. Both ready for religion, and in that case, we're out of line,' and as I say it – well, of course, the lines are curved, and Daria says,

'I could buy another house,' pointing to her bags and boxes, full of cash, around our feet.

'And we could live there,' Mara says, her cat's eyes round as suns.

'No,' says Daria, 'a little house, not big enough for you.'

'No, Mara, I can't put you up,' I say. 'I may go tracking through the stars, my Master calls,' although he won't. In all that space, to find Alessia, you'd need

to fiddle with the quantum – and in the end, it's clear
we two didn't suit.

'Mara,' I say, to comfort her, 'there's always
trains, they're full of wheedling folk who've left and
not arrived. Someone will take you in.'

We take our costumes off – they haven't served.

The oxen have their destiny in mind: they pull us
off the metalled road, and take a track. Around there's
starwort, and celandines. We hear aimless barking
from all distant sides. On a bush, there's draped a drab
flag, greyed out with sun.

'A smugglers' track,' says Daria, and to me,
'You'll know it well.'

'The time has come,' I say. 'It's upward – or its
backward, back to palaces and plots.'

'The guys have turned against us,' Daria says,
'It's strange, but maybe we should take account of
that...'

We reach a gate, the frontier.

The oxen push, it opens easily, and here there's geese
and little hills. And Mara asks, her thread of voice,

'Which country can this be?'

WASTED LIVES

You have to wait for something. Even if you're on the move, and running. Expect it; might be good, even if you're a fugitive, a refugee, or just plain bad.

It's a rich day, walking in the rain around the old town. There! – a black bird, diving in the swollen river. An honour guard with a flag, for monarchs, in their royal tombs. A funeral – some showbiz figure; the dark mourners, their concentration intense, quite moving. Dressed serious black, not in glitter. The white and gold – a Cadillac tourer – waiting outside for the brown box. Inside, the church, itself a brown box, mosaics of white sheep. Apostles. Us, sheep, they say we are. On every corner, talking statues, worn lumps rubbed down with votive exhortations, stroked by knotty hands.

The tea rooms and their smell of stewing cabbage. The porticos, the temples, the plastics of those deportations. Angry groups around a banner, remembering the executions.

I say to her, my friend, 'You know, we could find a hotel round here, an hour or two, to send the flame up high.'

'There!' she says, 'You've spoilt it, everything.'

We walk in silence, overhear – 'Oh no! Look at his lids, we'd never get justice from that one.'

'Shut up,' says the other, hurrying them away.

'He looks like Nero.'

'He's a judge, not justice. He makes his rule.'

Here, ranting on a corner, some old guy – talks about the bombing, ensconced in his dementia, guilty grin on his smooth face – it can't have been him, his memory; he wasn't even born, but now he's lost his past, can't even remember yesterday. Neat and clean – must be dressed by someone else.

'In the old times,' says the old man, 'the Marxists knew the truth about everything. And each one knew it in a slightly different way.'

'And those were the best days?' I ask, anxious to avoid offence, and not showing I was bored and awed.

'Yes,' says the ancient, 'and the communists ran a long ways after, trying to put things into practice.'

I ask, 'Where should I go, old sage, to start again? Also to hide?'

'Nature's the place,' he says, 'so long as you're inedible. No one will even sniff at you. You can take the train.'

Alone, I take the train. Time to be off and looking, far away.

THE WILDLIFE LODGE

'You saw the wild horses?' The manager is eager.

'Of course. No one looks after them.'

'That's the point. They started off dumped here. Did you see the little guys out hunting ostriches?'

'Absolutely not.'

'Well, the rest is television. We all do that, watch, the locals too.'

'I might stay here longer.'

'It costs. Do you have the cash, Caligari? Italian?'

'Greek. My parents ...' I say.

'You're too old to be one of the computer punks, you can't tell if they're good or evil, or just punks.'

'I don't hack. You can't travel if you're one of those.' He's not convinced.

'I'm a parfumier,' I say. 'I'm here to clear my nose. No resins here. Horse and people, their sweat, is all.'

I pull my nose a little, then some more, out to its fullest length. I smile at him, I fondle it a little, tilt it like a flute. 'You're not one of us?' I say. He turns away. 'It's a fine organ, this,' I say, and make to furl it.

'You hack,' he says, 'for sure. But why you came, it's all a mystery, like all the rest you've thought up. You think it gives you inspiration here, when there's next to nothing. Purity is not the way, is not how it's done.'

'I know,' I say. 'It's mixing the exotic stuff, and have it waft in bars.'

'You could steal something for me.'

'There's nothing there. It's in the air, The only real thing is the bottle, the shape, like hidden parts of bodies.'

He'll let me stay until I steal for him, and he finds my secret.

It's not at all like that.

Here's his woman, black and supple as a liquorice bootlace. No kids likely from that old black wire. An anomalous green sprouting? Not likely, not desirable. She looks at me eagerly.

'Give me your strong wrists, sir,' she says. All our food is in cans – you need some strength to twist it out. No sorcery in this kitchen.

'I'm a parfumier,' I say, to justify myself, and skimp the task.

'That's more your masturbation,' says the crone. 'You do it for yourself, not to please another. It's chords and gardens, there's no penetration, it doesn't leave a mark.'

'I need to clear my nose,' I say. 'I've seen the horses here – they're wrong. Without water, they all die.'

'It's the state,' she says. 'It's there to protect the rich. The rest – it doesn't keep marauders out. They come anyway. The armies only save and perpetuate the hierarchies.'

'Not many of those is coming here,' I say, trying to keep up with her. She doesn't believe my tale either. Caligari on safari.

'The ostriches,' she says. 'Their heads are down, but not to hide. They're listening ...'

'For that train from Yuma,' I say, pleasantly. 'It's true, I came by train. But you must wait for clients coming different ways ...'

'You'll stay here. Maybe you're not what I'm waiting for. But then, you'll have a message,' she says, hoisting herself on my arm. 'I hate those skinny brown guys, hardly a metre tall. They're all we've got. Harassing the ostriches ...'

'People come here to get away, not because they've got a special thought,' I say. 'In fact, their minds are empty, and they want them emptier.'

'No, no,' she says. 'It's for the sand. One day this will be a city like another, with towers and ruins. First it was gold, and then the water. So precious, but they've gone. Now, they'll want our sand. We've plenty. It will make our fortune, and there'll be a message and a messenger, then someone with a promise, who will save us from the things we've built – there always is.'

What does she want of me? What past has she planned for me?

'You were wanted back there,' she says. 'Up where the priests forgive you, and your comrades don't. You're a tall man, taller than the little brown guys here. Somewhere, there's wealth to do with you,' and on she rambles.

I say, 'You can't say here's unspoilt, not like they do. Apart from selling sand, and you've got lots, you need some plan ...' I make it like a question, as it's clear they've no idea.

'Some guys have learned to ride the horses,' says the crone: 'They round up people here and take them off. We should decide – should the horsemen take more off, or should we try to stop them.'

'It's safety,' I say vaguely. 'And reproduction. The apocalypse that burns off and regenerates.'

'History is a language, signs,' says the old black lady. Maybe she's young, instead. 'You see it when it's written down, or chiselled in. You don't feel it so when it is happening. The Germans, now – great linguists. They left the horses here, and now these short guys have to face the riders. At least they've got the television in the wait. The clients want to see the emptiness. It fills them up. So, carry off the short brown guys, the hunters! But – what if it's us that's left with emptiness?'

'You're the lucky ones,' I say, 'to have the choice, and either way is right.'

'And you,' she says, 'you have the choice – to do a flit, or stay, ingratiate – and either way is wrong.'

Why are these two here? I wonder. Maybe they'd kept a brothel, ran out of girls. Or wanted to invest. Now there's only the madam left – 'Yes, dear,' she says. 'Do call me Madam.'

And the man, the manager. I tell him, 'Nothing shady about me – just politics went wrong. Another language ...'

But – no. Languages don't go wrong – a sign, you can turn it round, point it the wrong way – but it's not 'wrong'.

'Have it your way,' says the guy. 'As for us – we came here through responsibility. Not guilt. To re-create.'

'What crap,' I think. 'It's all been changing, and for ever here. These brown guys – our ancestors' skulls on their shoulders – always moving up and down. Following the game. Stuck here and hunted. Do they want to make our beds? Open the cans, or clean the can? Want. That's the word on all our brows, one day should be hidden by those laurel leaves.'

'We had to leave the game,' he says. 'Peace!'

The game. The casino? Sex? Snuffing the competition? Banking? The Great Game?

His wife, his woman asks, 'You could have brought your girl?'

'Oh,' I say. 'I didn't know her well.'

'So what?' the woman says. 'That's not part of anything. Maybe you were special, that's why she thought you were a drip.'

'It's true,' I say. 'I had a role. I made collaborators, and I made resisters. That doesn't make me anything. We – they – could all be shits, or just striving to the light.'

'Crap,' says the manager. That's all.

I think, 'The Germans weren't just linguists, they were philolinguists, scientists. Lots of tongues, lolling out along the way. Them horses, not needed any more, just dumped and running free.'

We watch an opera on TV – Love's elixir. The production had them in a climber's camp – backslide of Everest; singing in Italian, they climb the magic mountain. Some sherpa lures them to their death, but love prevails – or was he selling snake-oil? We sit cosy, at a loss, unmoved.

'Love's always on the move,' the lady says. 'You need oxygen, though. And a push up the backslide.' She laughs, the manager takes a long gun and fires out the window into the black.

'I hope I don't hit a ridgeback,' he says. 'It's the wild ones I'm after. In the morning, there's nothing – any dead, they're eaten. Right up,' and he laughs too. 'Then another lot are there. But it's a thing you have to do.'

They stare at me. The manager says, 'You call me Anton. Anton. It sounds like Danton. I'm not that famous yet, maybe I'll never be.' He pulls his woman close, 'This is my crooked black cheroot, my Sylvie.'

So, this is true love. Getting the heights and colours right, at least. He's buff, yellow and supple as a Pomeranian trooper's coat.

'You have to take a side,' says Sylvie, peering at me without trust. 'But – you calculate. You want to build a wall. Instead, you are a part of one, a stone in the wall. Live or dead, once you're in among the other stones, it doesn't matter if you're live or dead.'

Bands of horses come to stare at the lodge: 'They're so thirsty,' Sylvie says. 'At night, there's dogs, of course. They could protect us.'

'And the ostriches?' I ask.

'They wait, they listen, and they hear the trains,' she says. Then, 'What happened to your women?' I improvise, I tell her,

'Ordinary things. They disappeared, or didn't stick. In Rome – a strange one, out of my league.'

'I could be one of them,' says Sylvie, as I'd feared. 'Now, you know everything about us. Anyone could find you here.'

'I've stopped being what I was,' I say. 'And I'd see them far off, unless it was the night.'

'Well, that's become your idea now. Waiting,' she says, dismissively. 'Like us. But selfish.'

She pushes me down the steps – layers of habitation once, all exhausted. 'What do you see?' she asks.

'There's black,' I say. 'And further down, more black. It might be infinity, or deep nothing. Up here, the dark, and down ... it's speculation. You could fall in, if there's an in, and drop. Or not.'

'If it were water?' Sylvie asks. 'Water beneath the sand, another precious stock.'

'You'd keep it for yourselves?' I ask. It could be water. Could be oil. Or air, as dark as dark.

'You find out, if I push you,' Sylvie says. 'A wash might help. Those sins. More too, wash it all down – "*le vin du souvenir*", that's what the poet says. Suppose that we don't know, no more than you, what's underneath? You could try a dive! And as for sex, my dear – it's not the duration, it is the intent. Have you the courage? Calculation? Even chancing progeny?'

'What a net you have there, Sylvie, casting it around,' I say. 'You bring it back – the world I've left

– the apartments unfurnished, full of bin bags, guys in meetings never sitting down, the fallings-out. The last guy's the one who gets hurt – the least deserving, just the most to hand. It's a diver's world – stay down too long you suffocate. Come up too quick – you bubble out.'

'I don't want to hear about crime,' says Sylvie primly. 'With us it was Germans. Leaving the horses when they'd done with them.'

'We had Austrians,' I say. 'Not many horses left, but we still use them.'

I hear her say to Anton, 'A big fish. Riches somewhere.'

Anton says, 'It wasn't just the Germans. It happened everywhere – the Great War: they dumped the horses and bought automobiles. How they cried, the riders, when they opened up the boxcars, let the horses out. It happened everywhere. The horses were delighted, didn't know this was a desert. Everyone still cries about it. They ought to.'

'Look,' says Sylvie. 'Enough with tears. This guy here,' she tugs at me. 'Maybe he can save the scene. We need to make some sense, some order. All the pieces here don't fit. The sand, the water – then there's nature – dogs and horses. Maybe they didn't want the dogs, and dumped them too. At any rate, they've ended here. Us waiting for the customers to take the train,

DOWN FROM THE STARS

come down and watch it all. What it doesn't do, is make a reason, resolution. It's just a puzzle to us.'

'There you've been,' Anton says to me. 'Being independent. Drugging, misleading, betraying. Keeping to your path, and not knowing about living. But knowing about keeping order, and escaping what is after you, to catch you.'

'Yes,' says Sylvie. 'Anton and I, we have each other, but we don't know about the outside, about making an order. We just survey the pieces.'

It's all hypocrisy, of course. How'd they make the cash to buy this place? Making frocks? If the cash was clean, buying here must be a fraud on them – you only come here to escape what you've been doing, too risky to go on, and Sylvie interrupts, 'Oh no. This was our dream. It turned out it didn't stick together, just like dreams may do.'

'The horses,' I say. 'That was a hundred years ago. The ones here, now, they can't think out a better place to go. They're stuck.'

'Horses don't see it so,' says Sylvie.

'A circus,' I say. 'I could bring it in – all girls from Colombia. I fell in love with each. It could be like opera in Manaus ...'

'No,' says Anton. 'That's not the order that she has in mind. They'd go off, the acrobats, their order or disorder going too. There's nowhere they can hang trapezes from ...'

'Well,' I say, '|there's poker. Order in that. A casino. Or love and sex – there's order there, and taking trains to anywhere, it all comes in.'

'No, no,' says Sylvie. 'That isn't it at all. It's using what we have, not ordering some others in. Unless they're clients, quite by chance, with empty heads.'

'The hunters here,' says Anton, 'they do the business – praying to the spirits, dancing the dance. But really – they'd wipe it out, everything, the animals – they're for ever whittling at the arrows. Passes the time. They're idle.'

'I've been big time,' I tell them. 'There's nothing I haven't done.' They're not impressed.

I hear Sylvie whispering, 'He doesn't understand at all. That's the way, like always – a guy who's done it all, he can't do something else.'

'If he's got cash,' says Anton, 'we'll take that, and have the riders carry him to wherever it is they go. When we say "order", he thinks harmony. Or unity! The creep!'

They cackle both. No, I don't understand at all, nor why they leave the blackness underground – they've not tossed down a stone, a hook, a net, and seen what came up, or what went down. Maybe they did.

I lie awake. Sylvie comes to me, she's supple as a trooper's overcoat. I hear Anton's gun, into the black outside, the dogs that never bark.

'And did you have sweet dreams?' asks Anton the next day. 'Here, you've seen – there's nature, all around. Some humans too, that make a kind of bridge. That's an unbroken membrane, joining everything, the universe, the past you can't remember and the past out there, where the stars are doing business, and everything's re-ordering, like the glass crumblies in kaleidoscopes. And here are we, who know the secrets, and the bigger one as well – to change the whole design. But – into what? That's what we sought from you.' He sighs. 'The clients are so few, and when they come, they disappoint. There's nothing but to give the bill.'

I say, 'It's curiosity they come with, and they take away. What more do you expect?'

He nods. I see that on the bill there's stuff I haven't had.

'You heard Anton, chasing away the horsemen, in the night?' asks Sylvie. 'They came express for you. That's what we have to charge for. Ammunition costs, you know.'

I say, 'I have a friend, a dancer, from the North. She always wanted to know what was coming next. And then it came. It never satisfied.'

'That dancing is a fraud,' says Sylvie, decidedly. 'They never listen to the music. They just count.'

I give them money. 'I may stay on,' I say.

'This money is no good,' Anton says. 'This comes from where you were. You made it up, this cash, it can't be changed,' and Sylvie says, 'We can't change anything, you know. That's what we've been telling you. There's only us and animals, and people in between.'

I pay a local – he has a pick-up truck. 'Quietly, quietly,' I say. 'The train.'

'They all leave this way,' he says. 'Off to the station.'

On the way, there's every kind of beast we see – the troops of elephants, ostriches on their *qui vive*: the horned, the tufted and the bald.

'Tell me,' says the guy, 'when you have seen them, the animals – what comes next? What do you do with them, the images? Is it knowledge that you seek? Or just more curiosity?'

I tell him that's what Anton wants to know, and Sylvie too. The answer satisfies.

He says, 'Call me Uwe. They left the horses, but gave our ancestors some German names we didn't want.' I say,

'You don't seem to want the horses either, Uwe. Why don't you shoot the animals with a gun, like Anton, if shoot you must?'

Uwe says, 'We can't shoot from horseback. How did you like the wildlife?'

I say, 'There wasn't much. It all seemed aimless like it does when there's humans too.' He says,

'I mean Anton and Sylvie – they're the wildlife, that's why the lodge is called that way. You try to tame them, though I don't know why. They don't understand the currencies. The clients never get to pay. That's why they're angry, anger like a black pit beneath their feet.'

'We're all angry,' I say, 'not just them, and other hungry animals. See – I have all the skills political. I don't need material, nor a settled price: just people. Eat, cajole, or forming fours – it's all the same, what I can do. Anton and Sylvie, though – they were tough.'

'Maybe you should have eaten them, however tough they seemed,' says Uwe, and he laughs.

'They make out, I guess, resist, survive,' I say offhandedly.

Uwe's suddenly angry – 'And us? Our land and our tranquillity? The balance quite upset, the firing in the night!'

'I just came to clear my nose,' I say. 'There's nothing for my perfumes here, just sweat. Your future – it will come, no doubt.' He doesn't offer songs or dance. He stares.

'This seems to be my train,' I say. 'My money doesn't buy a ticket, so I have the choice – on top, or underneath the seats.'

'The choice is dust, or wind,' he says. 'There's many names for different winds, but only one for dust.'

My! – look at the faces, curious ...

THE TRAIN

Here – is Tamara, Mara: 'I came to find you, and I've booked your place,' she says.

Oh no, I think: all kinds of sex are quite banal but – that pursuit by love is torment never written true, insatiable. Poor Mara, unrequited passions, empty as a wind ...

'I tried all others,' Mara says, 'and that left you. You'll take me in.'

The train leaves, if you're booked or not.

Here comes the scenery. Guys on horses, riding along a bit. You envy them.

'Caligari, the parfumier: that's excellent,' says Mara. 'It makes you think.'

'Let me sniff you, Mara,' I say. 'It could be bottled, the essential you – pickling the cabbage, smoking the fish. Diesel.'

'Forget the cabbage,' Mara says. 'We wander. Do no harm. It's when you settle – there come mudslides.'

'I'm clean,' I say. 'Right through, not just my nose. How'd the others do?'

'Everybody suffered terribly, now they are fine,' she says. 'Daria, the players and the bosses. I knew I'd find you so – you people seek a refuge, but it's really battles in nature fire you up. Impossible situations.'

I put my arm around her. 'Here come the cops,' I say. 'Romance should substitute my documents. And for sure there's exciting people on this train.'

We pass wood cities – and we think of Kurt Cobain, and where he came from; tin cities, brick and concrete ones.

It's all passé,' says Mara. 'All the countries and the states, the cities – no one wants to live in those and have some guy like you exploit them. Now, it's food and savings – eat, don't spend. That, you can do just anywhere. You stereotype me, so I'll do the same to you. Big fish like you are swallowed up by bears.'

194

I've no answer. I hear her say, 'You slept. You spoke of horses. Borne away by trains.'

I say, 'The cops don't trouble sleepers.'

'Russians bring horses in, to every writing,' she says. 'Horses suffer terribly, they aren't ever fine. And parasites, humans, on their backs, like ticks – horses make decisive gestures, just before they die, they're sacrificed. It's knowing your own tricks, it gives you depth, at the last.'

'It was Kant, spoke of the misery of horses. Besides, I'm not Russian, Mara,' I say. 'If anything, I'm an impresario. No tricks or laughter there. Seeing the cutting edge forever dulled, even as it cuts. Little poems, bellying out in music. Guys standing on each other's heads. The culture, Mara – some say it's made by gays, some say it's the voice of the oppressed. No, it's a tool, and I have been its sharpening steel.'

'That wasn't how it seemed,' she says.

'Don't flap those little wings, Mara,' I say, 'You're the kind that won't take off. You lay your lovely neck, so long and white, down in the sand, and wait, and listen to the distant feet.'

She doesn't care. 'I just want to express my being normal,' she says.

'Nonsense, Mara,' I say, irritated. 'You're an ice-queen. You're not normal. You just study what you think that is. Anyway, who wants it? Normal, it never did anyone good. You want someone to keep you, but you'd live on, dancing. Impossible! Look at me – I don't want to leave a mark. I am a mark.'

It's a discovery. When I say it, I know that's what I want. The rest is passé: being caught and being criticised. Falling down, being propped up. Being on a payroll. Rousseau and Kant – you're stuffed in their pillow, listening to their awful dreams, their sleep-talk, the classy snoring. This is passé too; it doesn't matter.

It's night, inside and out. Still we roll on.

'Your girl – losing her ... I can't imagine,' Mara says, at a loss.

'She casts her shadow, Alessia does,' I say. 'At night, it's all shadows, though the stars ... we say they shine. She's up there, light that can't illumine. Her mark, her dark light.'

Stars, like an equation blown to dust, quite useless.

'No,' says Mara. 'Not useless, just inexplicable.'

The train runs by savannahs, escarpments, volcanoes, the herds, the slums, the sand that one day we shall trade and fight about. It would take three murders, just to show one side is savage, and is serious. Our species seems to overdo: three would be enough to scare the others, but we multiply the killings, as if we're inexhaustible. I say, 'You never just run away. You run towards a better end.'

Anton and Sylvie – I think, 'I like them, they teach you nothing.'

Mara says, 'Look at the animals, all eating each other.'

There's nothing to see. Sometimes the train slows down, some guys toss out a mansized bundle. We meet no one, exciting or not, no guru, no fraudster. That's quite good.

Marx once applied for work, as a booking-office clerk. That's my link with him. The trains, the tickets, keeping my nose clean – no kids, no Mrs Marx to push me, either. Cajoling the travellers – to longer, ever longer journeys, Siberia, Vancouver, spreading the word, watching the scene, no home, casual contacts with the random. The hard carriages. The trolley with the samovar. The rootless – on and on, into every corner ... and Karl, sending them off, writing the tickets with his sharp steel nib.

Mara says, 'You'll be accused.' I'm startled, nearly fall off my stool, upset the ink, the gum, despatcher's world.

'Rubbish, Mara,' I tell her. 'I didn't mine, poison the wells or drink them dry. I brought novelty, avoided apocalypse.'

'No, no,' she says. 'We all knew there was apocalypse.'

'Apocalypse is judgment – end of the world's oblivion. I had the philosophical bent,' I say.

Our train pushes through the dark like Marx's pen. Mara says,

'Then there was Lenin's train – another long ticket there. You and I,' she says, her face excited, 'we'll burst upon them all – two lotus buds breaking open!

'I'm not so sure,' I say. 'The history may not bear your weight.'

'Then there's Tolstoy, Trotsky – at the end, they had to do with trains ...' she says.

'Mara,' I say, 'enough. The legend's in the journey, not being shunted into sidings. I have the thrust. Not the vision, maybe. Like the wildlife – like those two, Anton and Sylvie. Got to go beyond.'

There's white dots in the skies – not stars. 'Those swans,' says Mara, 'go together faithful all their lives.' I say,

'That's because they're indistinguishable, Mara: sleeping around just doesn't figure for those guys.'

'It isn't you,' she says. 'I love you, but I don't refer to you. Don't get puffed up. I need a stage to dance on, that is all.'

'It's the past, Mara,' I say, kindly. 'It sucks your blood. It kills you. Even the jobs you didn't get.'

Mara: fixed on me. She's a dumpy Siberian, one white metal tooth, the rest quite fair, she's paddling

out, into the lumpy waves of middle age. I don't tell
her so. I'm sure she knows.

'I know I'm not beautiful,' says Mara, 'but I'm
good.'

'That should make you happy, Mara, but you're
not. Maybe you're just good by instinct. Most people
don't even know they're good. Or don't want to be
happy. It's quite complicated,' I say.

I think of the sorcerer: he cured me – but he could
have saved the effort, just by warning me – 'don't
sleep under the blood-sucking tree.' There – that
would be easy. It's as if we're characters struggling
against their script.

'Let's not go back to where we were,' pleads
Mara. 'You made it sound so simple – but you didn't
even place it right.'

I'm irritated. She makes me think about Daria, and
I'd rather not: I say – 'You told me near your house it
was so cold, to start the trucks, they took out a plug
and used a stick of dynamite to turn the motor over.
Now, Mara, reflect. Does that seem possible?'

'I always believed it so,' she says. 'The cold is
legendary, quite attested.'

'This trip is over, Mara,' I say. 'I must summon
up another fortune.'

'You didn't make much sense when you were in
the arts,' she says. 'Sense of them, that is.'

'It was my mistake. I saw it all as wildlife. The subtleties escaped. Next time, I'll concentrate on nature. Bring on the animals,' I say. 'It's the traffic I'm good at. I was even popular, in my way.'

TERMINUS

Guys on rugs, lying around the station. Brewing a stew – cow's entrails, that looks like. If they were rated higher, you could form a gang at once. Lean faces, wolves from my country, lots of them.

Mara clings to me: 'Remember Daria?' she says. 'She's scared. Afraid they'll take her off. Her house....'

If you steal, you're always scared. I say,

'The answer is – sell me her house. For nothing. Under my name – Caligari, the good doctor, mixer of smells and spells. That way, she possesses nothing, cannot be accused.'

Mara's impressed, 'You know all about the law,' she says.

'I don't want a house,' I say. 'One that is hot. I want the cash, to start again. Maybe some traffic, bringing on the animals, leaving the art behind.'

'My, those entrails,' says Mara, joyfully. 'It makes me remember goat's udders, broiled. Our treat.'

I say, 'You may be right. Reason leads us to the good, but clearly that's a tricky thing – you don't have time to cogitate, you need the cash, the reasons clash, not everyone will join the game ... These guys, that lie around on mats, a past and future drab – they can't be organised in crime. Just hit and run is mostly what they do. I have in mind ...' and here I turn my nose towards the cooking smell – 'The broiling and the roasting, and the animals – they come together in a fragrance that strikes deep into your instinct. My! you think. How good! You bottle it, the smell. You do no harm. It's not like flowers that no one knows, the modern stuff that has no smell.' Mara says,

'It's not right. Not right for you. The idea may float on, and pull you in, but you attract the gangs that make you feel alive. That's your landscape, like an overcoat about you. You start from the foundations, making do. It's true – the wildlife's food. We'll eat those horses, and the ostriches. Someone will eat the dogs. We need to eat the wildlife, sooner or later, that's its destiny – its fragrance too. It's just – that you aspire to more important posts.'

'I'm in the world, Mara,' I say. 'That's the half of it – lightens up the rest.'

'These people,' she says, pointing to the bodies lying round, like troopers exhausted by retreat, 'These poor people, with their wasted lives.'

'You shouldn't say that, Mara,' I say. 'It's not over for them. Nor for you – see, in the end, you left your prison – and you'd done nothing specially wrong to get set there. It took some chutzpah to climb on the train. I was already in the world, and being there, that lets you out of many troubles. Nothing's wasted, Mara. It all gets eaten.'

'I'm a dancer,' Mara says. 'I was trained. You've no idea how hard that is.' We wander up and down.

'We must eat, Mara,' I say. 'I left from here, this city. It's not so easy.'

We look up at the stars: there's Alessia, hidden behind the glow from street lamps here below. There's my old mentor, somewhere, scrabbling at her with his paws. Science, just now, is no assistance.

'We'll eat and doss down with these guys,' I say, 'and then we'll start the climb again. Reasoning, make the ascent.'

There's always Wildlife Lodge, I could return and see those sawn-off ends of art and animals that Sylvie tries to fit together, Anton's long gun that keeps them separate.

It's burnt meat satisfies the gods, the stars, the starmen too. Those fine noses. The smoke, the charred cadavers, breaking the vital chain, and making things inedible.

I reflect, I compromise, I say, 'We'll put an act together, Mara. Like it was, out of remembrance of those guys from everywhere who came and brought us justice, improvised, gave us a boost, pepped up our lives.'

'Yes!' Mara says. 'But something new, not just the shards of shows gone by.'

The guys here, on their mats or under rugs, have quietened down.

'I'm hungry still,' says Mara. 'Tell me, how'd you get to eat? Where is this country's food? Can't we raise some cash? There's no one round to see me dance.'

I say, 'Mara, they'll come. They always do. They'll come to see the show. For certain, you will be a star. And I'll be one again.'

About the author

John Fraser has lived in Rome since 1980. Previously,
he worked in England and Canada.